"A KLINGON IS NOT BORN A WARRIOR!"

Gowron, leader of the Klingon Empire, addressed the assembled Starfleet officers. He pulled out his knife and stuck it deep into the tabletop. "Being a warrior is something that must be earned. Before I earned this knife, I owned a *ghojmeH taj*, a boy's knife."

Gowron glanced around at his audience for a moment. "This story is about Pok, son of Torghn, my friend and ally. A mere boy with a *ghojmeH taj*. I will tell you how Pok became a warrior. . . ."

Look for STAR TREK Fiction from Pocket Books

Star Trek: The Original Series

Star Trek: The Next Generation

Star Trek: Deep Space Nine

Star Trek: Voyager

STAR TREK®
KLINGON™

**A novel by DEAN WESLEY SMITH and
KRISTINE KATHRYN RUSCH
Based on the script by HILARY BADER—
Story by DEAN WESLEY SMITH and
KRISTINE KATHRYN RUSCH**

POCKET BOOKS

New York   London   Toronto   Sydney   Tokyo   Singapore

This book is a work of fiction. Names, characters, places and incidents are products of the author's imagination or are used fictitiously. Any resemblance to actual events or locales or persons, living or dead, is entirely coincidental.

An *Original* Publication of POCKET BOOKS

POCKET BOOKS, a division of Simon & Schuster Inc.
1230 Avenue of the Americas, New York, NY 10020

STAR TREK is a Registered Trademark of Paramount Pictures.

A VIACOM COMPANY

This book is published by Pocket Books, a division of Simon & Schuster Inc., under exclusive license from Paramount Pictures.

ISBN: 0-671-00257-0

First Pocket Books printing May 1996

10 9 8 7 6 5 4 3 2 1

POCKET and colophon are registered trademarks of Simon & Schuster Inc.

Printed in the U.S.A.

For Rich, Kelly, and Jeff

Authors' Note

This book takes place before Commander Sisko is promoted to captain. At that time the Klingon Empire and the Federation were still working together, at least in a limited fashion.

Chapter One

THE YRIDIAN PILOT smelled like an abandoned fish-processing plant on Balor 6. Layers of stink and dirt covered him and the raglike clothes he wore like coats of paint. He huddled his huge frame against a support pillar on the upper deck of the Promenade, trying to look as if he didn't stand out. But his odor warned anyone of his presence a dozen paces away.

He'd come to *Deep Space Nine* to make some money. Some very good money, as far as he was concerned. Enough for him to buy a new trader ship to replace the one he'd lost in a bungled smuggling operation with a stupid Ferengi.

He glanced around, watching the few humans below closely. A Klingon warrior strode purposefully along the railing of the upper deck. His knife clanked softly against his leg and he walked with a confidence only Klingon warriors had. As he passed the trader he stopped suddenly, then turned to face the Caxtonian. He wrinkled his nose and stepped back a full step. "Are you Kathpa?"

The Yridian trader nodded. "Are you—"

The Klingon warrior held up his hand for the trader to stop, then glanced around. The Promenade below had a few midafternoon shoppers, all humanoids. Not one seemed to be paying the odd meeting any attention.

"It does not matter who I am," the Klingon said. He reached into his breast pocket and pulled out a small wrapped package. He tossed it hard against the chest of the trader without coming closer. The package made a smacking sound as it hit and the trader caught it before it dropped to the ground.

"Your first payment," the Klingon warrior said, his voice low and firm. "If you fail, you will die. If you succeed, you will be rich. Make sure you do not fail."

The trader pulled the package into a hidden pocket in his rags and smiled at the Klingon, showing a full mouth of yellowed and rotting teeth. "I prefer being rich over being dead."

The Klingon snorted and turned away.

The Yridian trader watched him go for a moment, then moved away from the pillar, heading in the opposite direction.

After they were both out of sight, what looked to be nothing more than a painted bulge along the edge of the pillar a dozen steps away from where the meeting had occurred started to melt onto the floor. It soon re-formed into the shape of Odo, the changeling who served as chief security officer on *Deep Space Nine*.

Odo's earth-toned uniform and expressionless face formed with the rest of him. He glanced first in the direction the Yridian had gone, then in the other direction after the Klingon. "I don't like the sound of that," he said aloud. Then, at a fast walk, he started after the Klingon.

The patrons of Quark's bar had the feel of a crowd verging on being out of control. Quark was behind the bar. From where Commander William T. Riker sat at a large, empty table below the Dabo games, he could only catch a glimpse of the Ferengi and his big ears through the crowd pressing the bar for drinks. Rom, Quark's brother, looked as if he was about to burst into tears as he fought through the crowd with tray after tray full of drinks and empty glasses. Riker found himself feeling sorry for the small Ferengi. Quark always treated Rom like a slave instead of a brother. And with this many people in the bar, Quark continuously yelled at the smaller-eared Rom to do this or that task.

Rom almost dropped Riker's drink in front of him, then mumbled his apologies.

"No problem," Riker said, but the Ferengi had already turned and was scampering to the next table.

Riker took a sip and let himself savor the sweetness of his brandy while he looked around. The patrons of the bar were divided into fairly even numbers. A third were Klingons, most of whom had arrived with Gowron for the meetings with the Federation. The Klingons were making the most noise, talking and laughing the hardest and the loudest. Klingons not only fought with more gusto than humans, they drank and laughed more. It was one of the many things Riker liked about them.

Another third of the bar's patrons were Federation and Starfleet personnel, a large number of whom were also here for the meeting. The humans seemed to huddle in small groups, heads forward, talking almost in whispers. And all still wore their uniforms, just as he did.

The final third were Quark's normal alien customers, including Bajorans, two Cardassians, Yridian traders, and a host of others from a dozen races through the sector. They seemed to be paying the Federation and Klingon patrons no attention at all.

Normally Riker would have enjoyed the feeling of Quark's this evening. He liked a place that had an air of excitement to it. But with the meeting between the Klingons and the Federation going on here on DS9, the tension in the bar felt more dangerous, as if a war might break out at any time.

Riker sipped his drink and forced himself to relax. For the moment he was alone. And every moment alone these days was to be treasured.

Another sip and Riker saw that Captain Jean-Luc Picard, followed by Commander Benjamin Sisko, was slowly winding his way through the crowd toward Riker. Not far behind them was Commander Worf, followed by Chancellor Gowron, head of the Klingon High Council, Gowron's guard, and Rear Admiral Admiral Edward Jellico from the United Federation of Planets.

Jellico, unlike Picard, had a full head of gray hair. He was a tall man, standing a good six feet six inches. And he never seemed to smile. About halfway through today's meeting with Gowron and the two other representatives of the Klingon High Council, Riker wondered if Jellico had ever smiled in his life. When Jellico had been promoted to Admiral, Riker had hoped never to serve under him again.

For the first time since Riker's last run in with Jellico, Riker remembered just why he hated the guy so much.

Riker stood as the other officers joined the table, with Jellico luckily finding a chair on the opposite side, as far away from Riker as possible.

Riker turned his attention to the Klingon leader. Gowron had an air of power around him. He had pronounced ridges on his head, and his arms and shoulders were full and powerful. He was the best warrior in a culture of warriors. He had not gotten to that position by being either weak or stupid.

As if by magic, Quark appeared at the table just as Jellico finished pulling his chair up. "What can I get you gentlemen to drink?" His smile seemed almost real and Riker managed to keep his laugh to a faint chuckle. Quark, of course, served the table of important people. That was just like him. From this table he might gain something to make him a profit beyond the price of the drinks. He would never trust such a table to his brother.

"Blood wine," Gowron said, his voice powerful. He swept his hand around at the entire table. "For everyone."

Picard held up his hand and Riker again managed to hold back a laugh.

"Tea for me," Picard said. "Earl Grey. Hot."

"Nothing for me," Sisko said.

"Water," Jellico said. Then he glared at Quark. "And make sure it's pure."

Quark said, "Of course." And then smiled at the admiral.

Riker purposefully said nothing. He would accept Gowron's offer. He'd tasted blood wine a number of times. It wasn't a favorite of his, but he could drink it at special times like this. Besides, someone needed to accept the Klingon's offer, or it would be considered an insult under Klingon customs.

Worf also said nothing. It would have been an insult against Gowron for Worf, a Klingon, to turn down the offer of blood wine from the head of the Klingon High Council.

"Bah!" Gowron said, snorting at the humans around him. "Only Riker among you will drink with me. Such weakness. It is no wonder we disagree at the table."

Jellico glared at Riker, but Riker only continued to

smile. If the meetings weren't so important to relations between the Federation and the Klingon Empire, he would have enjoyed baiting the admiral even more. But now Jellico's lack of understanding of Klingon ways might just be another step toward a new war.

"My friend," Picard said to Gowron. Picard leaned forward and turned to face Gowron squarely. "It's the differences between us that we must learn to celebrate. The talks are simply to—"

A loud shout and a smashing chair broke off what Picard was saying. Riker instantly saw what was happening. Near the bar a Klingon had stood in anger, facing a group of Starfleet personnel at a neighboring table. Three other Klingons were also on their feet, and before anyone could do anything, the area erupted in a fight.

Klingon warriors and Starfleet personnel tangled in a mass of twisting color while Quark's normal customers backed away, their drinks held aloft to keep them from spilling.

"Stop!" Quark's shout could be heard over the noise, but no one paid him the slightest attention.

Riker jumped to his feet and Worf was right beside him.

Dozens of others around the bar also converged on the fight, as if everyone knew that this fight had to be stopped instantly, for the sake of the talks, if nothing else.

Riker waded into the fight, grabbed a Starfleet lieutenant and pulled him roughly off a Klingon. With a twist Riker spun the lieutenant away into the hands of other waiting Starfleet personnel.

Worf stepped in front of one Klingon and growled a warning, freezing the Klingon in midpunch.

Riker stepped into the center and shouted, "Stop it! Now! That's an order!"

The last of the struggling stopped as the half-dozen combatants on each side paused, all breathing hard. Almost as if by transporter Odo appeared at Riker's side.

"Go to your tables or the brig," Riker said, "Your choice."

The crowd hesitated.

"We demand honor," one Klingon said.

"Another time." Worf growled in his face. "This is not the place."

"Now!" Riker said, his voice firm. He wasn't going to allow a stupid bar fight jeopardize the important work of these meetings.

The Starfleet personnel stepped back and then a few of them turned back to their table as the noise level of the bar came back up to a normal dull roar.

The insulted Klingon glanced at Worf, then around at the table where Gowron still sat, smiling. "Bah," he said and spat on the floor. "Humans have no honor to defend." He turned back to his table and sat down, his back to Worf.

Riker, Odo, and Worf stood their ground until it was clear the combatants were back to their drinking.

"I think I will stay here for the moment," Odo said,

glancing first one way at a table, then the other at the Klingons.

Riker nodded. "That would seem like a good idea."

"Who is going to pay for the damage?" Quark demanded, stepping up to Odo and Riker while holding a broken chair.

"I'm sure," Odo said, "that your profits tonight will more than make up for a broken chair."

"But—" Quark started to object, but Odo stopped him.

"I could shut this bar down if you'd like, to find the person who broke the chair."

Quark glanced at the crowd around him, then at the broken chair. "I suppose," the Ferengi said, "I could write this up to the cost of doing business."

"Exactly," Odo said.

Riker laughed, and turned to see Lieutenant Jadzia Dax standing behind him. Her smile made him feel almost like a young boy again. He had hoped that Dax would show up tonight, but hadn't found a way to ask her at the conference today.

She stood almost tall enough to look him in the eye. Her hair was pulled back, and like the other Starfleet personnel assigned to the station, she wore a regulation jumpsuit instead of a standard uniform. Riker hoped that Starfleet command would eventually authorize this design for shipboard use. As he caught himself admiring both the jumpsuit and its occupant, he noted the smile on Dax's face went clear into her eyes.

"Commander," she said, nodding and continuing to smile. "Nice job."

Riker shrugged and indicated that she should join him back at the table. "I doubt it will be the last fight I break up this trip."

"I hope you're wrong about that," she whispered to him as they neared the table.

Picard saw her coming and smiled, moving over so that she could pull a chair up next to Riker. As they sat down Gowron was talking, obviously getting very frustrated with his Federation companions.

"Do you think we Klingons kill anything that stands in our way?" he said, sweeping his arm in the direction of the fight Riker and Worf had just broken up. "You outsiders see only our fierceness, our love of battle. You do not see the *tIgh,* the honor, that shapes our every act."

"In my observation," Jellico said, staring right back at Gowron, "Klingons look for the slightest excuse to fight."

Gowron glared back for a moment before Picard broke the silence. "Gentlemen, please. We are here to find ways to better understand each other's culture."

"My point, exactly, Captain," Gowron said. "Klingons are warriors. We do not fight *just* to fight." Gowron glared at Jellico, then turned back to face Picard.

"Admiral," Worf said, "Klingons fight for honor. The honor of the Empire. The honor of family." Worf glanced at Gowron, who nodded his approval, so

Worf turned back to the Admiral. "Sir, honor is all we treasure."

"We also fight for honor," Admiral Jellico said, "but most times we do not do so at the drop of a hat."

Gowron laughed, leaning back and letting the laugh break out over the table and the crowded bar as if he'd just heard the funniest joke on the station.

Riker knew what Gowron was laughing about. To a Klingon, humans had no honor. Jellico's claiming otherwise was a true joke to Gowron. And from what Riker had seen in his time aboard Klingon ships, and in his dealings with Klingons, including Worf, humans valued honor very little in comparison with a Klingon warrior.

"I don't understand just what—" Jellico started to interrupt Gowron's laugh when Gowron waved his hand for him to stop.

"Admiral," Gowron said, leaning forward and facing Jellico. "Klingons are good storytellers. Have you heard such?"

"I have," Jellico said.

"Good," Gowron said. "For I have a story that will give you understanding of Klingon warriors. I warn you, it is a long story. But I will tell it well."

Admiral Jellico glanced at Picard who nodded slightly.

"All right," Jellico said. "Tell us your story."

Gowron smacked his hands down hard on the table. "Good." He took a long drink of his blood wine and then motioned for Quark to bring him another.

Then, eyeing his audience, he sat forward.

"This is a true story." He pulled out his knife and stuck it hard into the tabletop. "A warrior's knife," he said, indicating the weapon. "But a Klingon is not born a warrior. Being a warrior is something that must be earned. Before I earned this knife, I owned a *ghojmeH taj,* a boy's knife."

Gowron glanced around at his audience for a moment. "This story is about Pok, son of Torghn, my friend and ally. A mere boy with a *ghojmeH taj.* I will tell you how Pok became a warrior."

Gowron glanced at the others around the table, then frowned. "But this will not do. No. Not at all. To tell this story correctly, I need someone who knows little of Klingons."

"Why?" Picard asked.

Gowron turned to Picard. "To answer my questions. This is a story of decisions. A warrior learns by such decisions. And none of you will suit my purpose. Do you have someone who might join us?"

Riker glanced around the crowded bar and his gaze came to rest on a group of engineers from the *Enterprise* drinking in a far corner. Lieutenant Barclay sat in the very corner, nodding to some conversation. His tall, too-thin frame seemed almost to swim in his uniform.

"Sir," Riker said, turning to Picard. "I think Lieutenant Barclay might be a good choice."

Picard looked almost startled, then smiled, glancing in Barclay's direction. "I think you might be right,

Number One." Picard glanced at Worf. "Please ask him to join us."

Worf stood and moved across the bar as Quark sat a new glass of blood wine on the table in front of Gowron.

"Ah," Gowron said. "Keep them coming, Ferengi. Telling a story is thirsty work."

Chapter Two

LIEUTENANT BARCLAY had been listening only half-heartedly to the conversation among the other engineers at his table as they argued about the best places to eat. Ensign Sutter insisted the best place was a cafe on Rigel, while Ensign Dern swore it was a five-star restaurant near Starfleet headquarters in San Francisco. Barclay didn't much care. Instead his mind was focused on a problem he and Chief Engineer Geordi La Forge had been working on concerning a modification of the warp coil. He'd offered the idea of a modification that would result in making the coil 6 percent more effective. Geordi had jumped at it. If it worked, Geordi would make sure he got the credit. And more importantly, maybe Geordi would then listen to a few of his other suggestions.

Suddenly the conversation at the table stopped,

leaving what felt like a hole of silence in the noisy bar. Barclay glanced around, but all eyes at the table were focused on a place over his right shoulder.

"Lieutenant Barclay," a deep voice said.

Barclay spun around and looked up at Worf. The big Klingon seemed to tower above him and Barclay's first instinct was to duck. But he managed to just nod instead.

"The captain asked that you join him."

Worf indicated the table where Captain Picard sat with Riker, Dax, Commander Sisko, Admiral Jellico, and the head of the Klingon High Council, Gowron.

"B–b–but, why would h–h–he—" Under pressure his stammer always seemed to get worse and this time was no exception.

"He is the captain," Worf said, his voice firm.

Barclay glanced at the frozen faces of the other engineers for help, but it was clear that no help was coming. Slowly he pushed back his chair and stood. He felt as if he were going to be executed. What could the captain want from him?

Worf only nodded and led the way.

The crowd in the bar seemed to part in front of Worf like water in front of a boat, and Barclay found himself staying close to the back of the huge Klingon as if being pulled along in his wake.

"Ah, Mister Barclay," Picard said as they approached. "I'm glad that you could join us."

Barclay wanted to say, *It seemed I didn't have a choice.* But he only nodded and took the chair Riker had moved into position.

"So this is the Barclay who will help me tell my story," Gowron said, leaning forward over the table to stare into Barclay's eyes. Gowron glanced at Riker. "Is he up for the task?" Then the leader of all Klingons turned his intense gaze back on Barclay.

Barclay wanted to shout *What story?* but instead just stared at Gowron. He'd never seen the leader of the Klingon Empire up close before. But Barclay had imagined that if he ever got the chance, he'd be scared. And right now he was terrified. Gowron had as powerful a presence as Worf. Maybe even more. And right now Gowron's blue eyes seemed to be cutting through to his very soul.

Riker slapped Barclay on the back while laughing heartily. "Of course he is," Riker said. "He's one of the smartest engineers we have on the *Enterprise.*"

Gowron continued to stare at him for a moment. Then he asked, "What do you know of my people?"

Barclay swallowed, shrugged off the sting of Riker's slap on the back, then shook his head. "N–n–not much, sir."

Gowron sat back, laughing. "He will be perfect."

Then suddenly, as if Barclay had made him angry, Gowron leaned forward, pulled out the knife sticking in the table in front of him, and stuck it back into the table in front of Barclay. The knife vibrated for a moment from the force.

"Do you know what this is?" Gowron asked, his voice roaring so much it almost covered the rest of the noise in the bar.

16

Again Barclay forced himself to swallow, then said, "A–a–a knife."

"A warrior's knife. It is mine."

Barclay nodded and glanced at Riker who was smiling at him. Riker nodded, so Barclay turned back to Gowron who had leaned back and was taking a drink from a large goblet, as if telling the truth about the ownership of the knife was the most important event of the day. For all Barclay knew at this point, it might have been.

Gowron wiped his mouth on the back of his sleeve and sighed. "My story is about Pok, son of Torghn, my friend and ally."

Gowron sat back and settled into his story.

"There was a great party in the house of SepIch, Pok's house. The large building barely contained the rich smells of roasting *TKnag* beast. The table was full of dishes of food and most of the hundreds of guests had arrived, filling the rooms with their laughter.

"Earlier that day, Pok, son of Torghn, brought down the largest *TKnag* beast ever taken in *chontay,* the ritual hunt. His *naOjej* was sharp and his bravery will be talked about for many generations to come.

"I attended the party as an honor to Pok, and to my ally, his father, Torghn of the house of SepIch. As I arrived, with my two guards carrying my *cha'nob* gifts, Torghn was introducing his son to the guests. Not wanting to disturb the moment, I stood in the doorway and listened.

"Torghn indicated the huge roasting *TKnag* hanging over the open pit in the center of a large round table. Two Klingon warriors pulled tender meat from its sides and stuffed the meat into their mouths, letting the juices drip down their faces to show their enjoyment.

"'Nothing tastes as good,' Torghn said, loud enough for all to hear, 'as the beast killed in the *chontay.*'

"He was right, and the crowd shouted their agreement, and after a moment Torghn held up his hand for silence. Then he turned to a tall, muscular young man standing near the entrance to the room and said, 'Here is the hunter himself. Pok, come.'

"Pok strode over and stood beside his father. His expression, I could tell from the door, was intent, yet happy. I remember my own *lop 'no* and how I felt. A warrior never forgets that moment, that pride.

"'Here is the boy,' Torghn said, indicating Pok, 'whose *naOjej* brought down the largest *TKnag* beast ever taken on this planet. I am proud to call him son.'

"Torghn slapped Pok on the back as the crowd cheered.

"Then Torghn went on. 'Tomorrow, after the Rite of Ascension, I will be prouder still to call him Warrior Son!'

"The crowd clearly agreed. Having Pok for a son would be a great honor for any warrior.

"Torghn raised his goblet. 'To my son, who has chosen to follow the path of his grandfathers. To Pok.'

"The shout *'Oapla'* echoed through the room along

18

with the sound of goblets smacking together. At that moment I wished I had a drink in my hand to toast my friend's son. So I stepped forward and spoke. 'It pleases me that I shall be here at my friend Torghn's side to watch his son become a man.'

"Torghn and Pok both turned to face me, and both smiled. Smiles that make even my cold heart warm just thinking about them. I did not know it, but that would be one of the last smiles I would ever see from my friend.

"Torghn stepped up to me and we grasped arms.

" 'Gowron!' Torghn said. 'Your presence does my house honor.'

" 'May the house always deserve it,' I said. 'I have brought your son the *cha'nob* gifts.'

"My guards raised their arms showing the gifts to Torghn, who smiled and bowed slightly.

"Then I turned to Pok and said, 'Honor me by taking them.' "

Gowron glanced around the table and then focused his intense gaze on Barclay.

Barclay felt at that moment as if running might have been the best option. But instead he stayed glued to his chair.

"Federation person Barclay," Gowron said. "If you were Pok at that moment, what would you have done?"

Barclay glanced at Riker, whose face showed no trace of emotion. He quickly scanned the others at the table. Only Admiral Jellico showed emotion, and it looked closer to boredom than anything else.

"Come, Barclay," Gowron said, his voice firm. "Indecision is like a disease with you Federation types. You think too much. There is a Klingon saying. "Act and you shall have dinner. Think and you shall be dinner." You understand? Now take action."

Barclay managed to swallow the lump in his throat enough to say, "I w–w–would s–step toward you."

Gowron almost came out of his chair. "My guards would kill you if I did not stop them! Fool! Your action would be seen as a personal challenge to me." Gowron leaned across the table and touched the handle of his knife, causing it to vibrate again. "And trust me, human. You would not want to challenge me."

Barclay stopped his head from nodding and said, "I would step forward and accept the presents."

A huge smile broke across Gowron's face. "Now you are getting the idea. Pok honored me by accepting and taking my presents. If he had not done so, it would have been a dishonor. Understand?"

Barclay found himself again nodding harder than he needed to.

Gowron took another drink and sat back. "Now, let me get back to my story."

"Pok took my presents from my guard. I must admit, with pride, that they were almost more than the boy could carry. But he managed as any good son would have done.

" 'My house thanks you for what you have given us, Gowron,' Torghn said.

"I waved his comment away. 'I, above all others, know what *you* give up for me. For the Empire.'

" 'When my ancestors conquered Taganika,' Torghn said, 'and set up rule over the planets in this sector, they did so in service to the Empire. But now, the Empire's needs have changed, and we must change with it.'

" 'Well spoken, Torghn,' I said to him. 'But others here on Taganika do not see things as you do, my friend. The ancient houses have ruled these planets for many years, and it has brought them great wealth.'

" 'That is a truth,' Torghn said.

" 'They may not be as willing as you,' I said, 'to give up their power.'

" 'For the future of the Empire,' Torghn said, 'we will sacrifice the planets our grandfathers conquered, and that will bring us great *honor.*'

"Torghn took a step closer to me after saying that, and my guards moved in his way.

"I pulled them away. 'Enough. Do you think Torghn would allow me to come to harm in his home? I trust the house of SepIch to protect me. Leave us.'

"My guards both hesitated, as they should, then turned and moved to stand position near the door. No matter what my words, they would not be far from my side.

"I put my arm around Torghn's shoulder and we turned to face the room. All of the guests had gone back to their conversations, and across the room I saw

K'Tar, Torghn's wife and Pok's mother. She was as beautiful as the first time I laid eyes on her.

"Torghn and I were on a mission together, honoring the Empire. The mission is now of little importance, but during that time we met K'Tar. We both fell in love, but I had rank over Torghn. She was mine if I wanted. But I knew Torghn's father had just died and he was returning to his family home to take control of the ancient house. I planned to continue in space, fighting as a warrior for the Empire. I had no place for a woman. So I let Torghn woo her.

"'Your wife looks well,' I said to Torghn.

"Torghn glanced across the room to where I was looking, and smiled. 'Yes. Do you now regret that you did not take her as a wife?'

"I laughed softly. 'My friend, she has brought you great happiness. And a son. There is nothing to regret.'

"Torghn and I turned and there stood Pok, still holding his presents.

"'What do you stand there for?' Torghn asked. 'Go put your presents down. Bring some food back with you.'

"As we watched, Pok moved along the long table of food and passed near K'Tar. But as he neared the table to place the presents, he tripped and dropped them.

"K'Tar turned to Pok with an annoyed expression and both Torghn and I both managed to restrain our laughter.

"But then from a side door stepped Vok. Vok, my

enemy. Torghn's hated neighbor. I always thought he seemed more Romulan in his honorless existence.

"Vok stepped forward and stood over Pok. 'It is hard to believe one so clumsy and slow is capable of hunting *TKnag.*'

"Torghn started to move forward, but I stopped him with a touch to his arm. This was not his fight at the moment. But it seemed K'Tar thought it was hers.

"'My son saves his skills for the hunting of beasts,' she said. Then glaring at him she added, 'and enemies.'

"Vok laughed. 'Our houses have stood door-to-door for generations. Must we continue to be enemies?' He moved toward K'Tar and made a motion to stroke her face.

"She growled at him, and then swifter than most warriors she drew out a knife and twisted his arm behind his back, holding the knife to his throat. Then, mimicking his words, she said, 'It is hard to believe one so stupid and weak is capable of running a Klingon house.'

"Vok again laughed, seemingly not bothered by the knife at his throat. 'Why, K'Tar. Flirting at your age. What will Torghn say?'

"Again I held Torghn's arm as she released Vok. Then speaking to Pok, but looking directly into Vok's face, she said, 'Throw this *veQ* out.'

"Pok stood and moved toward Vok, reaching for the unwanted guest.

"'*bIyem'a'!*' Vok said.

"Pok stopped short of grabbing Vok, but from

where Torghn and I stood we could tell he wanted very much to kill the man. And I had no doubt he might have been able to do just that. He was such a strong young boy.

"'The celebration,' Vok said, 'was declared a *lop'no*. You have invited the spirits of all our Klingon ancestors. Tradition dictates that all are welcome to the *lop 'no*. Even ancient rivals. Even me, K'Tar.'

"'*Chut Ouj,*' K'Tar said.

"'*Lug ratlh,*' Pok said, almost spitting his words at Vok."

Gowron glanced around at his audience in the crowded bar, then took another long swallow before facing Barclay.

Barclay had been afraid this moment was coming. He was starting to understand what his role in this story was to be. Gowron couldn't make fools of Commander Riker or Captain Picard or Commander Sisko or Admiral Jellico. And Lieutenant Worf knew the answers to Gowron's questions. So to tell his story, Gowron needed someone to run through the possibilities, to make his points to the others.

And Barclay was the unlucky one. Why hadn't he stayed back on the Enterprise? This never would have happened.

"Well, Barclay?" Gowron said, leaning forward. "Speak. If you were young Pok, what would you do?"

Barclay shook his head side to side. "I–I don't know," he said. "I–I–I don't unders–s–stand Kling-on."

"Bah," Gowron said, dismissing Barclay's attempt

to escape the question. "You don't need to understand our language to understand us as a people. Now
answer."

"I–I–I would turn to K'Tar," Barclay said, his
words rushing out.

"And challenge her? Your own mother?" Gowron
broke down into hard laughter not shared by the
others at the table. Finally Gowron looked up at
Barclay. "Pok is still a boy until the Rite of Ascension.
He must do what his mother asks without question
until then. Guess again, human."

Barclay glanced at Riker who looked almost
amused. "Pok sh–sh–should throw out the enemy."

Gowron again laughed, and this time Worf snorted
his disgust.

"So you think Pok, only a boy, should go against
generations of tradition, dishonor his ancestors by
ignoring the *lop 'no?*"

Barclay shook his head. "Pok should s–s–step
back."

"Now you have it," Gowron said, lifting his glass
and saluting Barclay in very much a mocking fashion.

"It seems it is getting late," Admiral Jellico said.

"Ah, Admiral, I warned you my story was a long
one. I have not even reached the death of my good
friend."

Picard leaned forward. "Gowron, would it be possible to continue this story tomorrow, after the meetings? I think we can all learn from your tale."

Gowron nodded. "As always, Picard, you speak
wisely. Tomorrow it is, then."

They all stood.

Barclay watched as they started to leave the table. He almost began to think he'd escaped when Gowron turned to him.

"Barclay. Tomorrow you learn how a Klingon boy becomes a warrior."

Picard and Riker both smiled as Barclay nodded. It didn't look as if there was any escaping this story for him. He was trapped.

Gowron slapped Barclay hard on the back, in the same place where Riker had slapped him. He staggered forward a step.

"Do not worry, Federation engineer," Gowron said. "Knowledge will not harm you this time."

Barclay only nodded, biting his lip against the intense stinging on his back. The knowledge might not hurt him, but the comforting might kill him.

Chapter Three

COMMANDER RIKER MOTIONED for Dax to wait for him a moment, then watched until Picard, Sisko, Barclay, Gowron, and Jellico were at the entrance to Quark's.

"I thought they'd never leave," he said, turning back to face Dax. "I was hoping we could have a nightcap." He indicated the now empty table littered with glasses and mugs.

She laughed. "With pleasure, Commander."

Riker felt his heart race slightly. He'd been hoping for years for some opportunity to spend time with Dax. It looked as if these long talks with the Klingons just might give him the opportunity, if Dax was willing. And so far she seemed to return his interest.

Riker scooted a chair out for her and then motioned for Rom to bring two glasses of wine. "I hope

Quark's best wine will do," he said as he sat down beside her.

"Very much so, Commander," she said, smiling at him. "What's the occasion?"

"Good company always requires good drink," he said.

She laughed.

"Didn't buy that, huh?" he asked, laughing with her. He really enjoyed her laugh and was glad she used it freely.

"Not for a moment."

Rom delivered the two glasses of wine and Riker waited until he had left before he held his up in a toast. "To a successful meeting."

Dax raised an eyebrow and smiled. "To success."

They both drank, then Riker turned to face her. "So what did you honestly think of the meeting today?" He watched her sip her wine and seem to ponder. He needed her opinion, because at this point he didn't completely trust his own.

"It didn't go well," she said, putting down her glass and facing him. "I think Gowron is intent on improving relations with the Federation, but I don't know how long that will last. And I think Admiral Jellico was the worst person the Federation could have sent to head these meetings."

"And why's that?"

She laughed. "Oh, come on. He hates Klingons. That much is clear from his every action."

Riker nodded. He'd felt the same way after today's meeting. And so had Captain Picard. But at the moment there didn't seem to be anything anyone could do about the admiral.

"I'm afraid I agree," Riker said. "But with the problems along the Federation/Klingon border heating up, and the Cardassians playing both sides of the fence, we need this meeting to work."

"Actually," Dax said, twisting her wineglass in her hand. "I don't think that's what is driving Gowron."

"So what is?"

Dax glanced around, then leaned in closer to Riker. "Gowron is barely holding on to power inside the Empire. There are many Klingons who wish the Empire had never stopped their conquering ways and they want to return to those old methods."

Riker shook his head. "They'd never stand a chance against the Federation. Not now."

"We know that," Dax said. "And so does Gowron."

Riker nodded. "So he needs the conference to help make relations with the Federation stronger so that if he needs to go to war against, say, the Cardassians, we might come in on his side. Or at least stay neutral."

Dax nodded. "But there are those on both sides who don't want this conference to work in any fashion at all. In fact, the very existence of the conference, whether anything comes of it or not, is bad for many."

This time it was Riker's turn to lean in closer to Dax. He liked her soft smell and wished he was leaning in at that moment for a different reason. "We have information," he said, "that there will be a Klingon disruption of the conference. Possibly an attempt on Gowron's life."

Dax looked him in the eye, not totally surprised but obviously taken aback nonetheless. "If Gowron is killed here, it might be taken as a dishonor by the Federation against the Klingon Empire."

"Afraid so," Riker said.

"Have Odo and Commander Sisko been informed?"

Riker nodded. "And security is everywhere. See the two drunks at the bar?"

Dax turned around to stare at the backs of two humanoids dressed in raglike clothing, sitting at Quark's bar. They looked like miners right out of the Conway mines. At the moment Quark was making a face at one of them, as the humanoid seemed to be passing out in his drink.

She turned back to Riker. "You're kidding?"

He shook his head. "We've got every area we can think of covered."

She glanced back at the two drunk miners and shook her head. "Amazing."

As she downed the last of her wine Riker asked, "You ready for another?"

She shook her head no. "But dinner tomorrow after the meeting would sound good."

Riker could feel the smile straining his face. "I'd love it. Another chance to talk."

She stood. "Until tomorrow, then?"

He stood with her. "Tomorrow."

Then he watched her as she left the bar.

"She's a hard one to not stare at, huh, Commander?" Quark said as he bent over beside Riker and started clearing the empty glasses from the table.

Riker laughed. "Yeah, you could say that." He finished the last of his wine, put the glass on Quark's tray, and headed for a good night's sleep.

With the meeting, followed by dinner tomorrow, he might need it.

Commander Sisko watched as Chancellor Gowron beamed back to his ship and Captain Picard beamed back to the *Enterprise*. Then Sisko turned to face Ops.

The current shift seemed to be going normally, considering the extra staff on duty. With two Klingon Birds of Prey and the *Enterprise* stationed off the station, all shifts needed extra help. And by the time the five days of this conference were finished, it would strain his people to the limit. And him, too. Today's meetings had exhausted him.

Major Kira Nerys seemed to be the only staff member out of place, since she wasn't scheduled for this shift. She sat at the security console, staring ahead. He excused the detail that had accompanied them to Ops, and moved her way. She didn't hear him as he approached.

"Sleep might be a good idea," he said.

She started, then glanced up and smiled. "Just making a few last-minute checks on station security."

Sisko nodded. He had the same worries she had. There was more than one rumor about an assassination attempt. And he didn't want it happening on his station.

"Any changes?" he asked.

Kira turned and indicated the board in front of her. It showed the positions of the thirty security personnel currently on duty. That didn't count Odo, who Sisko figured would be working every minute he could over the next few days.

"All seems normal," she said.

"But—?" Sisko said.

She glanced up and smiled again.

"I could hear it in your voice," he said. "Do you have anything?"

She shook her head and stared at the panel. "Nothing concrete. Just a feeling. A very bad feeling."

"So do I, Major," he said. "So do I."

And for the next half hour the two of them went over the tightest security measures ever placed on *Deep Space Nine*.

Chapter Four

QUARK'S BAR STILL SEEMED EMPTY compared with the previous evening. It was dinnertime and the day's meeting between the Klingons and the Federation had only broken up a little more than an hour before. The bar wouldn't get crowded until later, well after the dinner hour.

Commander Riker and Lieutenant Dax had left the meeting together and sat at a corner table, talking softly, laughing somewhat louder. Quark had served them his best dinner and wine and then, at Riker's pointed suggestion, had left them alone.

Two tables of Klingons filled the center of the room and three of Quark's regulars were at the bar. The noise level was high, but not enough to disturb conversation.

The Caxtonian trader Conpap strode into the bar and went directly to the back table where he sat alone. The night before, Gowron and the others had used the same table. He'd picked it purposefully, knowing that this evening the leader of the Empire might return to it.

"You know," Quark said, fanning his hand in front of his face as he stood in front of the Caxtonian trader, "that bathing might be an idea you should consider." Quark stepped back. "There are people eating in here."

Conpap just growled, then looked up at Quark and said, "Romulan ale. I am in a hurry."

Quark rolled his eyes and moved away, leaving the Caxtonian trader alone.

Conpap's gaze darted around the room, noting each person. Only three Starfleet crew were in the room, and he also knew that one of the customers at the bar was a security officer. He studied all of their movements, noting when they looked around and when they looked away.

After a minute Quark returned with his ale, slid it onto the table, and quickly left. Conpap pretended to drink, then placed the glass down. With one hand in his thick coat pocket, he pulled out a small bomb and pressed it firmly against the underside of the table.

It stuck there and no one seemed to notice. His hand moved away from the bomb no larger than the size of the base of his ale glass. He knew it had enough explosive to destroy this table and everyone at it.

He pretended to take another drink, then pushed

the glass to the center of the table and stood. He let one hand slide carefully into his pocket to the bomb's trigger, holding it like a prized toy. Later, when this table was again full and Gowron was entertaining the Federation people, Conpap would come back to the bar and, from a safe distance, set off the bomb.

And then he would be rich. Very rich.

A foolproof plan.

Riker finished the last bite of his steak and pushed the plate toward the edge of the table. "I think Quark outdid himself this time." He couldn't remember a meal that he'd enjoyed as much, both for taste and for company.

Dax smiled. "You didn't believe me when I told you Quark's had some of the best food on the Promenade." She leaned forward and whispered, "Just don't ask where he gets his recipes."

"Not a chance," he said, wiping his mouth and tossing his napkin onto his empty plate. He sipped his wine, letting the smooth taste fill his mouth and accent the lingering memory of the steak.

"You seem peaceful," Dax said.

Riker laughed. "Wonderful food and great company makes me relax."

She raised her glass in a toasting motion. "I'll take that as a compliment."

"As it was intended," he said.

Another sip of wine and he leaned forward. "You think today's meeting went as poorly as yesterday?"

Dax nodded, finishing the last of her Tautean salad

and pushing the plate aside. "I can't imagine that anything will—" She broke off her sentence and glanced up at something behind Riker. She had suddenly become very, very serious.

Riker turned around. Behind him Odo stood squarely in the middle of the entrance to Quark's. Four security personnel flanked him.

All four had their hands on their phasers.

Odo's gaze was across the bar and looked very intent.

Riker followed the gaze in the direction of a Caxtonian trader who was just moving toward the door. The huge creature in dirty pants and a ragged coat had just stepped away from the large table they had all sat at last night.

The Yridian saw Odo and stopped cold.

Suddenly the huge Yridian looked like a trapped animal. His posture tensed, his eyes went wide. Riker had seen that look more times than he wanted to admit.

The trader glanced one way, then another, obviously looking for a way out. Finally he made up his mind and darted to the left, just as one of the Klingon warriors at the center table pushed back his chair and stood.

The Yridian, his attention focused on Odo and the guards, bumped squarely into the Klingon from behind.

The Klingon spun, mostly on reflex, and pushed the trader backward into the large table.

The trader went down hard.

The next instant an explosion shattered the room.

Riker was slammed back against the wall, his head banging against the hard surface.

He felt the thud and then a flash of light and pain.

And then the world went black.

The next thing Riker knew, Dax was bending over him.

He blinked the dust out of his eyes and stared at her, forcing himself to focus on her face until the spinning slowed. She had a scratch across her forehead and her hair was covered with dirt, but she looked all right.

"What happened?" he managed to say.

She shook her head and glanced over her shoulder. "A bomb at the table we were at last night. It looks like it destroyed the back half of Quark's."

"The trader?"

"Dead," she said. "And possibly a few of the Klingons. I couldn't tell."

That wasn't going to help the conference. He tried to move and pain shot through his head, making Dax's face and the ceiling behind it spin like a ship out of control.

"Go easy," she said, holding him firmly. "You got a nasty bump on the back of your head."

He relaxed. Then he felt himself smiling through the pain.

"And just what's so funny?" Dax asked.

"I was hoping I would end up in your arms, but not this way."

She laughed and didn't answer.

But he could see the twinkle in her eye and suddenly his head felt much, much better.

Chapter Five

RIKER STOPPED IN THE DOOR to Quark's bar and stared. It was amazing to Riker how fast a Ferengi, worried about losing profit, could clean up a bar half-destroyed by a bomb.

After the blast Riker had beamed directly back to the *Enterprise* to have Dr. Crusher look at his head wound. She'd kept him in sickbay for an hour, then released him. By the time Riker had changed and gotten back onto *Deep Space Nine,* Odo had done his investigation and Quark had cleaned up his bar and opened for business.

It wasn't as crowded as last night, but getting close. Chancellor Gowron, Captain Picard, Dax, and Admiral Jellico were already sitting at a table against the back wall. A dozen Klingon and Federation security men stood around them, backs to the table, obviously on guard.

"How are you feeling, Number One?" Picard asked as Riker approached the table.

Dax smiled at him and indicated that he take a chair beside her. That made him feel even better.

"The head isn't ringing anymore, and Dr. Crusher said I will live if I take it easy for a day."

"Good man," Gowron said, slapping the table so hard he rattled the glasses and made two of the Federation guards flinch. "Hate to lose a Federation man who actually drinks blood wine like a Klingon warrior."

Picard laughed, but Admiral Jellico only snorted and sipped at his water. Beside him Dax lightly touched his arm to show she was glad he was all right, then moved her hand away.

"So what happened?" Riker asked after he got seated, glancing over at the area where the explosion had happened. A black stain on the floor was the only sign left of the incident, and Quark had placed a table over it in an effort to pretend it hadn't happened. No one was sitting at that table.

"The Yridian planted a remote-controlled bomb on the underside of a table," Dax said. "When he was bumped, he must have triggered it. Or his falling against the table did the trick. There wasn't enough left of him to be sure."

"Any clues as to who was behind it?" Riker asked, glancing around.

Jellico and Picard's faces both stayed purposefully

blank. Gowron waved his hand in dismissal. "I have enemies. It is the way of this position. I would rather get back to my story from last night. Where is that Barclay?"

Picard tapped his comm badge. "Picard to *Enterprise.*"

"Go ahead, sir," Data's voice came back.

"Have Lieutenant Reginald Barclay report to Quark's bar on the station."

"He is already on his way, sir." Data said.

"Good. Picard out."

"So he comes willingly." Gowron said. "Good, I admire a man who faces what he clearly does not like."

"Glad to see you feeling better, Commander," Quark said, moving in behind Riker's left shoulder. The Ferengi slipped a glass of wine in front of Riker. "On the house." Then, almost as if embarrassed by his actions, he moved quickly away.

Dax laughed, staring after Quark. "That's not something you see every day."

"I'll bet not," Riker said.

"Ah," Gowron said. "He is here. Now we can start."

Riker glanced around to see Barclay and Commander Sisko enter the bar and weave their way toward the table. It took them only a moment to be seated.

"Barclay," Gowron said, pulling out his knife and holding it. "Do you remember where we left off yesterday?"

Barclay glanced at the knife, then nervously nodded. "Y–yes, S–sir. Young Pok had just honored his mother's command to step back away from Vok, h–h–his enemy."

Gowron beamed. "Wonderful. A smart student. You will go far, boy." He leaned forward and jammed the knife into the table in front of Barclay. It stuck there, quivering.

Barclay stared at it, his eyes wide.

Riker bet that Quark didn't much like his customers doing that to the furniture, but it was Gowron, so what could he say?

"The task becomes more difficult with tonight's story," Gowron said. "So listen closely and learn of the honor of a Klingon warrior."

"Remember, when I stopped my story I was standing with my friend Torghn. His wife K'Tar had just told young Pok to back away from Vok, enemy of the Torghn's house. And no friend of mine, either.

"Vok half bowed to K'Tar. 'I knew you would not dishonor your House,' he said. 'I accept your welcome.'

"K'Tar snorted and almost spat at him. 'Vok, do not confuse tolerance with welcome. You may stay, but keep clear of my husband and Gowron. Do not spoil the day with politics.'

"Vok again bowed a slight, almost ironic bow. 'A pity,' he said, 'I did not bring my wife. T'Var could learn so much from you about Klingon hospitality.'

"With that he turned and went into another room,

away from my sight. K'Tar growled after him, then turned to young Pok who now stood over the dropped presents. 'I will see to these. Your father asked you to get food for Gowron. Now go.'

"I noticed that the table was full of the best Klingon foods, as it should have been in a house run by Torghn. Gagh worms, Rokeg blood Pie, heart of Targ, Bregit lung, and others. It makes my mouth water just thinking of such food.

"Young Pok hesitated a moment, then picked up a dish full of gagh, my favorite. I do not know how he had such knowledge. But his choice pleased me.

"I took the dish offered by the young boy and moved into the dining room with Torghn. Torghn's younger brother, Qua'lon bowed and welcomed me and together we moved to a table.

"Young Pok hesitated, not certain if he should sit with the men or move to the end of the room where the women and younger children were eating.

"I offered him a chair near his father. 'Sit.'

"But for a moment the young boy hesitated, as he should have done at such a moment.

"'Do not look as if you have tripped over a woman,' I said. 'Sit.'

"'Yes,' Torghn said. 'Sit.'

"'A woman?' Qua'lon said, laughing as Pok sat down. 'I doubt he knows what to do with a woman.'

"Everyone laughed for a moment, then I said, 'Enough joking. Soon one of us will go too far and find a *ghojmeH taj* at our throats. Open your *cha'nob,* boy.'

"Torghn nodded to K'Tar who went and retrieved the presents. She first handed Pok a large book, bound in a fine hide. Pok took it, a puzzled look on his face, and broke the seal. Inside it contained a musical score.

" 'Do you not know what that is?' Qua'lon asked.

"K'Tar laughed. 'The young are ignorant of their family's history.'

"Qua'lon looked at me, a sad expression on his face. Then he turned back to young Pok. "It is a score to *Qul tuq*. Can it be you have never heard the opera that tells the tale of our family's house?"

"Then Qua'lon began to sing, and for the next few minutes his wonderful deep voice filled the house.

"When he finished he turned to Pok, who still looked a little puzzled.

"Qua'lon turned to his brother Torghn. 'The boy is ignorant.'

"Torghn sighed. "Perhaps I have spent too much time teaching him to hunt, and not enough teaching him to sing."

"I waved the two brothers to silence and turned to Pok. 'The next. Open another.'

"Pok was handed a second present. This one had my metal seal around it. I had watched as that seal was placed on the box.

"Pok took out his knife and broke the seal with a flick of his wrist, then put the knife on the table in front of him. He pulled the lid off the box and I watched as his face came alive with pleasure. Carefully he reached into the box and took out the Acta crystal.

" 'That is as useful as latinum, young Pok,' I said.

"Torghn sat forward staring at the crystal, then looked up at me. 'My friend,' he said. 'The crystal is bigger than—'

"Suddenly something else came out of the box in front of Pok. Something I had not put in that box. The item was the size of a fat human cigar. It lifted out of the box and hovered over the table."

Gowron looked around at his audience in the bar and smiled. "Does anyone know what that object might have been?"

Picard nodded. "From your description," he said, "it sounds like a Romulan assassin probe."

Gowron slapped the table hard, smiling. "Very good, Captain. It most assuredly was an assassin probe hovering right in front of the young boy, Pok."

"So what happened?" Admiral Jellico asked. Riker glanced at him, surprised. It was the first time the admiral had seemed interested in Gowron's story.

Gowron gave the admiral a stern look. "My friend Torghn yelled out, *"HoHwI'"* A hunter killer. *petaD!"*

Gowron turned to Barclay. "Young sir, pretend you are Pok. In front of you hovers an assassin probe, moving, searching for its programmed target. You have a knife and the crystal in front of you. What would you do?"

Riker almost laughed out loud at Barclay's look of

panic. It was clear he had no idea even what a Romulan assassin probe was, let alone what Pok might be able to do to stop it.

"I–I–I think Pok should grab the knife," Barclay said.

Gowron laughed, then stared intently at Barclay. "You think you can defend against a *HoHwI'* with a *ghojmeH taj?* Your knife against a Romulan hunter killer probe? No, you must stalk it as it stalks its prey. Now, what would you do?"

Barclay looked directly at Gowron, then said, "I–I don't know what an Acta crystal is. Should I pick it?"

Gowron shook his head. "A mere trinket. Nothing of note when a Klingon is about to die."

Barclay nodded.

Riker took pity on the lieutenant. "Barclay," he said. "A hunter killer probe is programmed for a specific target. Stopping it always causes it to explode."

Barclay nodded and Riker could see the look of thanks in his eyes. It was clear Barclay hadn't gotten much sleep last night worrying about this session.

Barclay turned back to Gowron. "I would freeze in position until I saw the probe's intended t–t–target."

Gowron nodded. "Correct. Freezing is an action." He took a deep, long drink of his blood wine, then motioned for Quark to bring him another before he settled back into his story.

"I have no idea how the probe was placed into my package for Pok. But it took only a moment before it became clear I was the target. The probe seemed to hover, moving back and forth until it stopped, aimed directly at my heart.

"I was prepared to die. And at that moment I expected to.

"The assassin probe suddenly started at me. I moved to the left, but I moved too slow. However, my friend Torghn did not. He leapt in front of me, taking the probe into the center of his chest.

"He fell, faceup, on the table.

"My momentum tumbled me to the floor where my two guards covered me. By the time they let me up, Qua'lon had reached his brother's side and had put his ear to Torghn's chest.

"After a moment he looked up at me and stood. 'He did not even see the face of his enemy.' "

Silence ruled the table at the back of Quark's bar as everyone stared at Gowron. He took a sip of his blood wine, his thoughts far away.

Riker glanced at Dax, then back at Gowron.

For the next minute no one interrupted the leader of the High Council's private thoughts.

Chapter Six

PICARD GLANCED AT ADMIRAL JELLICO as Gowron sat in silence. Jellico seemed to be thinking. Picard hoped so. Jellico needed to understand that Klingons had emotions, feelings, friendships, and honor. Their emotions might be expressed in different manners from humans, but they were very much an honorable people. The Federation would be stronger having the Klingons as friends. But it was Jellico's blindness to that fact that was clearly the stopping point in the meetings.

Gowron understood Jellico's blind spot and was obviously staging this story in the hope of accomplishing here in Quark's bar what he couldn't get done in the official meetings.

And Picard would do everything in his power to help him. And Picard had no doubt that even Barclay understood the importance of the story he was playing a part in.

Gowron sat forward. "I will continue."

"Qua'lon, standing over his brother's body, did what any Klingon warrior would do. He demanded vengeance.

"'Do not let vengeance cloud your mind,' I told him. 'There is a ritual to be performed. Vengeance will wait for that.'

"Qua'lon looked at me, the shock and pain clear. He growled very low, then said, 'You are right. I will—'

"I interrupted him. 'No. It is not your place.'

"At that moment we all turned to face Pok, the young boy who had just lost his father.'

"It was Pok's place, as Torghn's oldest son."

Gowron sat forward, looking at Barclay. Picard didn't envy the young lieutenant's position, facing the head of the Klingon High Council. Picard had done so, and he knew the power of Gowron. And right now all that power was focused over the knife at Barclay.

"Do you understand," Gowron said, his voice low and mean, "what has occurred?"

Barclay nodded but said nothing.

"Then what should young Pok do? His father, dead on the table. His father's brother demanding vengeance. I also stand there in the crowd waiting for the young boy's decision. Should Pok move toward me, toward his uncle, or go to his dead father?"

Barclay glanced around the table, hoping for help. Picard made his face stay blank. He knew the right answer, because he knew Klingon rituals. But Barclay would have no way of knowing. Gowron was clearly testing him for a reason.

"M–m–move toward you?" Barclay said.

Gowron shook his head no. "I know the scene of death I have described is shocking to you humans. But the cowardliness of this assassination shocks even a Klingon's heart. Do not be confused by this. Approaching me at that moment would be deemed a challenge and an accusation that I was responsible for Torghn's death. I would have had to kill young Pok if he had done that."

Barclay visibly shuddered. "Th–th–then I sh–sh–should not pick Pok's uncle, either?"

Gowron smiled. "You are right. You should not. It would also be a challenge. Pok should go to his father's body for the death ritual."

Gowron took another drink and sat back, his voice level as if telling a part of the story he would rather not have told. Picard understood. He'd witnessed one Klingon death ritual and he hoped he'd never go through another.

"Young Pok moved toward the body of my dead friend. Torghn's eyes were closed and Pok leaned over his father. With one hand Pok opened his father's eyes. Then, moving so that his nose almost touched his father's, he looked into Torghn's eyes.

"Slowly, the young boy soon to be warrior let out a

low moan. It grew in intensity and as it did so the rest of us joined in.

"All of us.

"Men.

"Women.

"Children.

"We all moaned the loss of a great warrior until it became a great cry to the skies.

"I moaned the loss of a good friend. A friend of mine. A friend of the Empire.

"Then the loud death yell stopped.

"We stood in silence. Torghn's arrival with the Black Fleet had been announced. There was nothing more we could do. His soul had left his body.

"I moved to Pok and pulled him away from his father's body. Then I pulled out the killer probe and studied it. As I had expected. Romulan. A coward's way to kill.

"'It would have killed me,' I told them, 'if Torghn had not taken the full force of the probe.' I said what all knew, but I wanted to be sure my debt was clear.

"K'Tar touched her husband's hand, then turned to me. The look in her eyes would have stopped a charging beast. 'Was the seal on the present broken?'

"I placed the probe on the table, picked up the box. 'No,' I said, studying it. 'Yet I sealed the *cha'nob* myself, days ago. Long before I left for Taganika.'

"Qua'lon picked up the probe and studied it. 'A cowardly way to kill. No Klingon would use such a method.' With disgust he dropped the probe back on the table and Vok picked it up.

"'I wish I could agree,' I said to Torghn's brother. 'But the days when that was true are gone. There are too many Klingons who would use such methods today.'

"I watched as Qua'lon's eyes narrowed. Then he said, 'Vok!' He spun around to face his neighbor.

"Vok still held the probe, but he had taken it apart. He glanced up at Qua'lon. 'A clever device. And so effective.'

"'Vok!' Qua'lon said. His voice had a level of firmness in it I had not heard before from him. 'Your hatred of Gowron and my brother are well known.'

"'True,' Vok said, not looking at me. 'I would weep for neither. But there is no proof that—'

"Qua'lon grabbed the disassembled probe from Vok's hands. 'You have destroyed the proof.' He tossed the remains of the probe on the table next to Torghn's body.

"'What?' Vok said. It was clear he did not understand Qua'lon's thirst for vengeance.

"'Vok, you *verengan Ha'DIbaH!*' Qua'lon said. He stepped toward Vok. 'I shall have revenge on you and your house.'

"Before Vok could defend himself, Qua'lon drew his knife and plunged it into Vok's stomach, holding it there until the Klingon closed his surprised eyes and died.

"Qua'lon pulled out his knife, letting Vok's body drop to the floor. Then he turned and placed the bloody knife on the table in front of young Pok.

"'This is the knife,' Qua'lon said to Pok, 'that

killed the man who killed your father. I give it to you
to show the circle of vengeance is closed.'

"I leaned forward and picked up the knife.

"Qua'lon turned to face me, clearly stunned.

"'I understand the passion of your actions,
Qua'lon,' I said. 'I too have killed for vengeance. But
the circle of vengeance is far from closed.'

"Qua'lon stood in front of me, stunned.

"Finally he spoke. 'You saw yourself. He tried to
destroy the probe. Vok condemned himself. He killed
my brother.'

"'Yes, but think, Qua'lon,' I said. 'Vok is a small
man from this provincial world. To place an assassin
probe in *my* belongings would be impossible for a
single man. The package was tampered with long
before it got here. There were others involved. Now
that Vok is dead, we may never know who they
are.'

"I could tell Qua'lon was clearly stunned at my
words. But he also realized I spoke the truth.

"'I do not regret what I have done,' he said. 'But
you are right. There are others involved. The circle is
not closed.'

"I turned away from Qua'lon and moved to a place
beside the body of my friend. 'I will swear an oath. A
blood oath. To find all who are responsible for the
death of my friend.'

"'I will join you,' Qua'lon said.

"I held up my hand for him to stop. 'No. You must
stay here. Protect the House of SepIch. Vok's house
may seek revenge of their own.'

" 'But—' Qua'lon started to protest, but I stopped him.

" 'No. I need allies here. It will have to be another who joins me.'

"I picked up Torghn's knife by the blade. I closed my hand around it hard until it cut through my palm and the blood felt wet between my fingers. Then I took the knife away and slapped my bloody hand down hard on the chest of my dead friend.

"I held my hand there and looked around. 'Who will swear a blood oath with me?' "

Gowron sat forward and pulled the knife out of the table in front of Barclay. He held it in his hand and asked, "Barclay? It is time for young Pok to make another choice."

Barclay nodded. But before he could say anything, Admiral Jellico broke in.

"You said the man Vok was killed for vengeance? Was he ever proven guilty of a crime?"

Gowron laughed. "Admiral, you jump ahead of my story. But I can tell you this. Vok was later proven to be involved in the cowardly death of Torghn."

Gowron turned back to Barclay. "You have had time."

Barclay again glanced around and the simple glance angered Gowron.

"Bah," he said. "Humans and their need to think before acting. Klingons learn the opposite when they are children. When your brother says, 'Do this' then you do it, or you poise yourself to fight."

Gowron paused, then looked at Riker. "If a woman bares her teeth at you, you hold her off, or poise yourself to love." Gowron turned his attention back to Barclay. "Either way, the path is action. Consequences are dealt with later."

"B–b–but action requires knowing," Barclay said. "I–I–I don't even know Pok's choices of action."

Gowron laughed. "Two choices, Barclay of Starfleet. Swear or do not swear the blood oath."

"H–h–he would swear."

"And that he did do," Gowron said.

"I felt pride in young Pok at that time. He took his father's knife, cut his palm, and placed his bloodied hand on mine on his father's chest.

"His grip was firm. His hand hard. Not that of a child's.

"With me he repeated the words.

"'I swear on the river of blood in my veins. Vengeance on those who killed my friend, my father, Torghn! *Quapla!*'

"All the others around us shouted '*Quapla!*'

"And the oath was sworn.

"Then Qua'lon stepped forward. 'Wait,' he said. 'Pok has yet to complete the Second Rite of Ascension. In the eyes of the *nugh tlhegh,* he is still a boy. Would you have him seek vengeance before he has become a man?'

"'No, Qua'lon,' I said. 'I will not take a boy on a man's voyage. Tonight we will complete the Rite of

Ascension. Then we will seek out those who killed your brother.'"

Picard watched as Gowron stopped his story and took a long drink of blood wine. Admiral Jellico seemed interested at one moment and disgusted the next.

Picard found it all fascinating, not only for Gowron's story but for the fact that he was telling it here, at this conference.

Chapter Seven

THE LIGHTS ON THE PANELS were the only light on the bridge of the Bird of Prey. It hung in space over Qu'nos the homeworld of the Empire, waiting. Ten other ships waited with it.

Waited for news of Gowron's death.

The wait had lasted for days and the humor had left the ships.

The communications officer turned from his panel to face the command chair. A woman sat there. Another stood at her side. They were both dressed as Klingon warriors. Knives hung from their belts. Knives that had known blood.

"There is a message coming in," the officer said. "Coded Deep Space."

The woman in the command chair sprang to her

feet. "The moment is here," she said, moving around to stand above the communication panel.

"Do not be so hasty, B'Etor," the other woman said, also moving to the panel. "We do not know the nature of the news."

"I trust dRacLa, son of Vok," Lursa, of the House of Duras, said. "His hatred for Gowron is as sharp as mine."

"The message!" B'Etor demanded of the warrior at the panel.

He turned slightly, his shoulders almost showing fear for what he must say. "Gowron lives. dRacLa says the trader he hired failed in the task. He personally will try again."

B'Etor turned and smashed her fist into the pillar.

Lursa stood, staring at the main screen showing the homeworld below, obviously thinking. She and her sister were so close to taking control of the High Council. Only Gowron and his supporters stood in their way. He had to be removed.

Assassinated.

There was no other way.

And assassinated while meeting with Starfleet would only help the House of Duras.

After a moment she moved back to the command chair. "Contact the *BotKa*. Have it come with us. The other ships are to remain here."

She again glanced up at the homeworld.

"Sister," B'Etor said, moving to the side of the command chair. "What are we doing?"

"I am tired of waiting for others to do our work."

"As am I." B'Etor said. We go to *Deep Space Nine?*"

"Yes, we go to the Federations," she said, staring out at the world below. "I have a plan."

All B'Etor said was, "Good."

Riker watched as Gowron took a long drink of his blood wine, then smacked his lips together. There seemed to be more of the story left to tell tonight. Even the admiral didn't seem to be in a hurry to leave. Around them the bar had filled with customers laughing and drinking. The Dabo table seemed also to have a lively game going and Riker wished he had the time to try it. But there was no way he would miss any part of Gowron's story.

"Admiral," Gowron asked, "have you attended a Klingon ritual?"

Jellico shook his head no. "I have not."

"Pity," Gowron said. "Captain Picard would tell you they are full of richness. Our rituals come down to us through centuries of tradition. They still serve us well."

Picard nodded in agreement.

The admiral said, "I can understand that."

"Good," Gowron said, smacking his wine goblet down hard on the table and looking at Barclay. "Young Pok had a very important ritual to go through after his blood oath. As I tell the story I will not bother to ask you for decisions. Only a Klingon would know the answers."

Riker laughed as Barclay breathed an audible sigh of relief.

Gowron smiled at Barclay. "For a human you do well. Do not worry. There will be more questions later."

This time everyone laughed as Gowron sat back and took up his story.

"A ring of stones framed the ritual chamber. A fire burned high in the middle of the room on a stone hearth, its flickering yellow fire the only light. On the walls hung Klingon weapons. Warriors' weapons. The night air sharpened the senses. A special evening. There was no doubt.

"Four Klingon warriors held pain sticks. Three were Pok's uncles. One from my ship. They stood two by two, forming an aisle to the flame.

"Young Pok entered the ring of stones and Qua'lon and I went to greet him, stopping two paces short of him. He was dressed as a warrior that night. His confidence gave him the courage to do so before the ceremony. I honored him for that.

"'Are you ready, Pok, son of Torghn?' Qua'lon asked. 'Do you wish to take your place among the great warriors of your house? Argan, son of T'lak. Seegath, son of Seeth. Janar, son of Seegath, Torghn, son of Kmpok. If so, step forward.'

"Pok took one large step toward Qua'lon.

"Qua'lon smiled, as did I.

"'Not every man has the courage to become a warrior,' Qua'lon said, continuing the ritual. 'Not every man can make the voyage through the River of

60

Blood even after he chooses to try. Will you make this voyage, Pok, son of Torghn?'

"Pok stepped forward again. He now stood face-to-face with Qua'lon.

" 'You have chosen,' I said.

"The four warriors in the gauntlet snapped their pain sticks as a sign of honor.

"Qua'lon leaned forward, speaking to Pok in a fatherly fashion. 'The night before your father's Rite of Ascension I lay awake, but Torghn slept soundly. In the morning I asked him how he had been able to sleep so well. He said, "My fathers and fathers before me have traveled the River of Pain. I know that the courage is in my blood, and I am not afraid." '

'Come,' I said to Qua'lon. 'It is time.'

"Qua'lon and I picked up our pain sticks and moved to our positions across from each other at the end of the gauntlet. Now Pok faced a line of six Klingon warriors, three on each side.

" 'Show us your heart,' Qua'lon said to Pok. 'Today you are a warrior.'

"Pok squared his shoulders and stepped between the first two warriors, never taking his eyes from the fire in front of him.

"The warriors on both sides of him used their pain sticks to shock and beat him. For a moment young Pok stumbled backward and I feared for him. But then he slammed back at their attack, kicking and fighting them until he had moved to the safe area before the next two warriors.

"Across from me Qua'lon nodded his approval. I

agreed. Pok had done well so far. He had fought back against the pain.

"The young Klingon took a deep breath and stepped between the next two warriors. They were even more savage than the first, as was their duty. They jabbed him with the sticks, kicked him, smashed him with their fists.

"But Pok fought back, deflecting their blows, moving with others. He stepped past them and they bowed in honor to his courage.

"Now he faced only Qua'lon and myself.

"I could see the determination in his eyes. He never looked at us, only at the fire in front of him.

" 'The battle is yours!' Qua'lon shouted. 'Travel the River of Pain.'

"Pok stepped between us and stopped. Qua'lon and I both took our pain sticks and pressed them against Pok, holding them against him.

"He trembled with the pain, but kept his feet.

"We pressed harder.

"He remained standing, his eyes focused on the fire.

"Finally Qua'lon said, 'Pok, when you die, you will die a warrior, and join the Black Fleet, where you will fight and die forever.'

"Qua'lon and I both pulled our pain sticks away and bowed to him in honor of his achievement. Pok took the last step through and stopped, facing the fire.

"His knees faltered and he went to the ground on them. But his gaze never left the fire in front of him. His back never bent.

"I stepped between him and the fire and said, 'It is finished. You have done well, Pok.'

"He looked up and saw me, then smiled. Beside me his mother rushed in and helped him back to his feet.

"'In one day's time,' K'Tar said, 'the House of SipIch has lost one warrior and gained another. You do us honor, Pok.'

"She bowed her head slightly, showing Pok his new status as the head of the house.

"Pok turned to me.

"'I see it in your eyes,' I said. 'One who has traveled the River of Pain. Others will see it too, and they will know that you have chosen the way of a warrior. And they will be afraid. That, too, is a weapon.'"

"Pok nodded his thank-you and leaned against his mother. I knew I had a strong new ally to replace Torghn.

"As we stood in the ritual chamber, giving young Pok a moment to recover his strength, one of the servants rushed in and whispered in Qua'lon's ear. He immediately turned to me. 'Gowron, your men have finished analyzing the probe.'

"'Come,' I said. 'Let us see what they have found for us.'

"We all moved inside and gathered around the dining room table. Tellot, my best science officer, sat at the table, the probe in parts in front of her.

"'The probe,' she said, 'was most likely manufactured in the Soltaris System, within Romulan-controlled space. The probes are illegal in almost all known sectors. Efficient. Deadly accurate, but difficult to program correctly, and even more difficult to come by.'

"'Unless you are a Romulan living in the Soltaris System,' K'Tar said.

"Tellot shook her head no. 'Even then. The materials for this one alone would bankrupt a small house.'

"Qua'lon turned to me. 'Gowron. Do you think there are Romulans involved?'

"'No,' I said. 'The Romulan want my *defeat,* not my death.' I turned to K'Tar and the rest in the room. 'Many things are difficult to come by, but nothing is impossible if you know where to look. I have not traveled through the dark reaches of space without learning where the dishonorable wretches do their dealings.'

"'Yes,' K'Tar said, 'and you have brought the fruits of their dishonorable hatred into this house.'

"I stared at her. 'Do you blame me, K'Tar, for your husband's death?'

"'No. But I entrust you with my son's life. Do not treat it carelessly. I too, can swear a mother's blood oath. You would not want that.'

"'No, I would not.'

"I held her gaze for a moment, then turned away. We understood each other. We always had.

"I walked over to Pok. 'Do not come because others want you to. You must know your own mind. Will you come?'

"'The boy has no choice,' K'Tar said. 'I have told

him the story of Kolan and Dula. Kolan let his father's death go unavenged. No one would marry him. He died without sons. His house became bankrupt. His name disappeared with the wind. Death is only death. My son will go.'

" 'Yes,' Qua'lon said. 'He will go.'

"Qua'lon turned to Pok. 'If you die for yourself, for your family, I shall have an opera written, just to tell the tale of your courage. Men and woman will sing the name Pok, *torghen puqloD.*'

"I laughed at them, and turned back to Pok. 'Your thoughts. Your own mind.'

" 'I have sworn a blood oath,' Pok said. 'I will travel after the murderers of my father.'

"I nodded. 'Have your things beamed to my ship. But do not take much. A farmer's treasures are a warrior's burdens.'

"Tellot stepped forward. 'Gowron, if we take the *BortaS,* the ship will be recognized long before we arrive. They will know that Gowron, head of the Klingon High Council, is coming.'

"She was right.

"Qua'lon stepped forward. 'Take my ship. Take the *Tagana.* Use it to find my brother's killers.'

"I nodded to him. 'Thank you, Qua'lon. I am honored.'

"I turned to Pok and my officers and guards. 'Come then. We have smelled the prey. Now let us follow the trail.' "

* * *

Gowron pushed back from the table and stood. "This seems a good place to end this evening. Tomorrow, if you are interested, I will tell of the chase of my friend's murderers."

"I would like that," Captain Picard said.

"So would I," Riker found himself saying.

"I, too," Admiral Jellico said, "would be honored."

Picard raised an eyebrow at the admiral's comment.

Gowron laughed. "Then tomorrow it shall be, after dinner."

He turned, and with his guards flanking him, moved across the bar and onto the Promenade.

Admiral Jellico, Captain Picard, Commander Sisko, and Lieutenant Barclay followed, leaving Riker standing next to Dax.

"I'm sorry dinner was interrupted earlier," Riker said.

"So was I," Dax said, smiling at him. "Maybe we should try again tomorrow?"

Riker smiled back at her. He had been hoping she would say that very thing. "With pleasure," he said. "It will give me something to look forward to during the long hours of the meeting."

"Me too," she said, smiling at him. "Me too."

And her words kept him smiling all the way back to the *Enterprise*.

Chapter Eight

PICARD FELT ANNOYED for the first time this trip. He remained seated in his chair as the rest of the attendees stood and left the large room. The round table was littered with water glasses and a few scraps of notepaper. For the third day in a row, the meetings between the Federation and the Klingon Empire had gone poorly. Both sides claimed they wanted to work with the other, yet there seemed to be no common ground on which to base trust. Tomorrow was scheduled to be the last day, but at this point Picard doubted it would even be worth his time to attend. Nothing was going to be solved.

"Captain?" Commander Sisko said, moving to a place beside Picard's chair.

Picard pushed his chair back and stood. "Yes,

Commander," he said, doing his best to keep annoyance out of his voice.

"My chief of security thought it might be a good idea to include you in his afternoon briefing." Then Sisko added quickly, "If you have the time."

Picard nodded. That made sense. Worf had been informing him as to what measures were being taken, but it would be good also to hear what Commander Sisko's people were doing, especially after the attempt on all their lives yesterday.

"I can make the time," Picard said, smiling at Sisko. "Lead the way, Commander."

Three minutes later he was seated in Odo's office, facing the changeling. Also there were Major Kira Nerys, Lieutenant Worf, and Commander Sisko. Worf and Kira remained standing.

Odo started in immediately. "It seems likely that the person directly behind the bombing was a Klingon named dRacLa. He's been on the station for three weeks, ostensibly working on an agricultural exchange."

"Has he been picked up?" Worf asked.

Odo shook his head. "No. Even though I witnessed a meeting between him and the Caxtonian bomber, we do not yet have enough direct evidence to hold him."

Worf nodded. Picard could tell he clearly wasn't happy.

"Any information as to motive?" Picard said. "Whom he might be working for? Or if he is working for anyone?"

Odo shook his head no and consulted his padd. "dRacLa is from the agricultural planet Taganika. He—"

Both Picard and Sisko said, "Taganika?" at the same time.

Startled, Odo looked up.

"Who was his father?" Picard asked. He had a hunch he knew.

"Vok," Odo said after glancing at his notes. "DracLa, son of Vok."

Picard glanced at Sisko, who looked as shocked as Picard felt. It seemed Gowron's story might have a little more to do with the meetings than Picard originally thought.

Riker and Dax left the meeting together, with Dax leading. She said she knew of a small cafe that was the farthest point from Quark's bar on the Promenade. "We won't be bombed there," she had said, and Riker had found himself laughing.

It had been some time since he had so enjoyed the company of a woman. Of course, Dax was not a normal woman, with all the Trill lifetimes inside her. But that made her all the more interesting. And mysterious.

The restaurant turned out to be a very small Argainian café with a wonderful wine selection. Huge plants hung everywhere, and small glow-pots on each table gave the entire place an intimate, yet outdoor feeling. Riker felt extremely comfortable by the time they were seated.

Conversation at first stayed mainly on the hopelessness of the meetings. They both very much wanted them to work, but like the rest of the attendees, they could come up with no place to really start.

They were halfway through the second course, a delicious Argainian soup, when Riker's comm badge brought Captain Picard's voice to the table. "All senior officers report to the conference room."

Riker tapped his comm badge. "Understood."

Dax shook her head, but Riker could see she was laughing at the humor in the situation. Twice they had been unable to finish a dinner together.

"Seems I am wanted elsewhere," he said, taking her hand. "Later in Quark's for Gowron's story?"

"I'll save you a seat," she said.

He nodded, then with a quick turn left the restaurant.

Five minutes later he strolled into the conference room. Captain Picard stood near the front of the table behind his chair. Counselor Deanna Troi, Lieutenant Worf, Data, and Chief Engineer Geordi La Forge were already seated.

"Sorry to pull you away from dinner, Number One," Picard said.

"No problem, sir," he said, and moved quickly around and took his chair beside where the captain stood. Beside him Deanna smiled at him with one of "those" smiles and he hoped his face wasn't red.

It took only a minute for Picard to fill them in on

the discovery of the Klingon dRacLa's history and his presence on the station. Riker was completely shocked at the news. He had been totally engrossed in Gowron's story of young Pok, but he had had no idea that a continuation of the story might be playing out as Gowron was telling it.

"At this point," Picard said, "we will not mention to Gowron that we know of the family history of dRacLa. Gowron and his security advisors have been informed of dRacLa's presence on the station. That is enough."

Picard looked at Riker, the only other person in the room attending the storytelling sessions, and Riker nodded his agreement.

"Now," Picard said, finally sitting down. "Commander Sisko is putting Deep Space Nine on alert status. This ship will go to alert and stay there until further notice."

Riker sat forward, puzzled. "Percussion only. Or do you expect trouble?"

Picard smiled. "I don't expect it, I *know* it's coming. I just don't know from which direction. And to start, two Cardassian ships will be arriving here within ten minutes. We do not know their mission or their intentions."

"Cardassian?" La Forge said. "They hate Klingons."

"And the Federation," Riker said, starting to understand where the captain was heading.

"Exactly," Picard said. "Disrupting these meetings

benefits any number of races, as well as factions inside the Klingon Empire. The Cardassians would profit greatly from a Federation/Klingon war."

"But I understand, sir," Data said, "that the meetings are not going well. Why disrupt a failed meeting?"

"Just the simple fact that the meeting is occurring is a bad sign for those seeking power in other ways, Data," Riker said.

Picard nodded. "Even if the meeting fails to come to any agreements, we need to guarantee it continues the full five days."

Everyone nodded and Picard stood. "Dismissed."

Riker sat for a moment longer, thinking, as the others filed out. Gowron must have known that dRacLa was on the station when he arrived. What was he trying to tell them with his story? Only Gowron knew. The rest would find out as the story progressed.

"Crafty," Riker said to himself as he stood. "Very crafty."

Chapter Nine

MAJOR KIRA STOOD next to Commander Sisko and watched on the Ops main viewscreen as the two Cardassian ships took positions a distance away. The *Enterprise* was off the port side of the station and Gowron's ships were on the opposite side. Kira felt surrounded and she had never liked that feeling.

"Hail them," Sisko said. His voice was firm, almost angry. "And make sure the *Enterprise* and the *BortaS* both are getting the transmission."

Kira knew how Sisko felt. With the meetings going poorly, the last thing the parties needed was the Cardassians poking their nose in.

"On screen," Ensign Hoffper said.

Gul Dukat's face filled the screen, and Kira snorted. Of course it would be him. He seemed to always know exactly when his presence would cause the most problems.

"What can I do for you, Dukat?" Sisko said, his deep rich voice full of power.

"Why, Commander," Dukat said, smiling into the screen. "Maybe I should be asking what I can do for you?"

"I won't play games, Dukat."

Dukat sat forward and Kira had the extreme urge to fire a phaser blast at the screen. But she held her position and her stern face.

"The entire sector knows," Dukat said, "that meetings between the Federation and the Klingon Empire are occurring on your fine station."

"It has not been kept a secret, Dukat," Sisko said.

"But the Klingon Birds of Prey headed your way have been," Dukat said.

Sisko stared at Dukat's smiling face.

Kira could feel the surprise building inside her. If Dukat spoke the truth, who knew what might be coming.

Sisko asked, "Is such an event your business, Dukat?"

"Commander," Dukat said. "It is bad enough that the Federation controls our station. Having the Klingons own it would be intolerable. I am here to make sure that doesn't happen."

Sisko laughed, his voice full and deep. "Dukat, you may stay in position, wasting your time for as long as you might like. But none of your men will be allowed

74

on this station until the meetings between the Federation and the Klingon Empire have ended."

"You're welcome," Dukat said, still smiling.

The screen went blank.

Kira turned to Sisko who stood for a moment staring at the blank screen.

"Do you think that he was telling the truth?" she asked.

Sisko shrugged. "His own form of the truth, maybe. There may be extra Klingon ships headed this way. Possibly Gowron's enemies."

Sisko glanced down at Kira. "But Dukat's motives have me confused," he said. "They make no sense. And *that* is not normal for Dukat."

Kira felt a chill run down her spine. On that, Sisko was exactly right.

Riker wasn't surprised that the large table against the back wall of Quark's bar had been held open again for Gowron and those who listened to his story. Two Klingon guards and two Federation security officers stood duty over the empty table in the crowed bar. Four men with weapons guarding an empty table. It would have looked humorous, if it hadn't been so important.

All of the members of the table arrived at almost the same time. After the Cardassian's surprise arrival, it was concluded by Captain Picard, Commander Sisko, and Chancellor Gowron that they made no difference in the evening.

Or in the meetings.

Gowron swore he knew of no other Klingon ships headed toward the station, but agreed to look into it. Maybe, he had said, the Cardassians were doing him a favor. Either way he had also agreed to continue his story.

Personally, Riker was glad that Gul Dukat's accusation of other Klingon ships heading toward the station was ignored, at least for the time being. There was no extra preparation that could be done. At least, no reasonable ones that weren't already done. Both the *Enterprise* and *Deep Space Nine* were on alert status. Gul Dukat clearly wanted to disrupt the meetings, and there was no point in letting him.

Dax touched Riker's arm and smiled as they all took their seats. Maybe tomorrow they'd finally have a chance to finish a dinner. He'd ask her after Gowron finished his story.

Quark appeared at the table as Admiral Jellico finished taking his seat. "Everyone drinking the same this evening?"

Gowron laughed and looked around the table. "Have any of you changed your mind on my offer of blood wine?"

Picard, Sisko, and Jellico all shook their heads no.

"Bah," Gowron said. "A good story is better told with blood wine. You do not know what you miss."

Riker had to admit that after two nights now of sipping the blood wine, he was slowly developing more of a taste for it. He still would never order it on his own, but it wasn't as bad as many in the Federation thought.

Quark scampered away as Gowron pulled out his knife and again stuck it into the table in front of Lieutenant Barclay. He focused his intense blue eyes on Barclay. "Young Pok is now aboard a ship I command."

Barclay nodded. "I–I–I remember, sir."

Gowron smiled. "Good. When the wine comes, I will start. There was much for young Pok to learn."

Riker managed not to laugh at the terrified look on Barclay's face.

Quark and Rom both brought the round of drinks and Gowron took a long draft, letting out a deep sigh when he was finished. Then he took a smaller drink, sat down his glass, and started into his story.

"Qua'lon's ship, the *Tagana,* did not compare to the *BortaS* in room and speed. But it was a sound ship. My men worked quickly to prepare it for the journey.

"The command chair filled the center of the *Tagana*'s bridge. There were stations for five others. I strode onto the bridge and knew at once it would be a good ship.

"Young Pok followed me and we were greeted by ChaqI, my weapons officer.

"'*DevwI,*' she said. 'The *Tagana* is prepared. We await your orders.'

"'Show me the weapons array,' I said. Then I turned to young Pok. 'You. Wait here.'

"ChaqI led me to a station on the lower level to the

left of my command chair. There she showed me the weapons of the *Tagana*. Again, not as powerful as my flagship, but useful.

"Behind me I heard SvaD, one of my guards, turn to Pok. 'Come here,' he ordered the young warrior. I later learned he wanted Pok to hold a panel while SvaD worked."

Gowron leaned across the table at Barclay. "One of many places young Pok is faced with a decision his first hours on my ship. Barclay, what should the young warrior do?"

Barclay seemed caught off guard with a question so early in the evening's story. But as Riker watched Barclay recovered quickly. "H–h–he should follow your order and wait."

Gowron roared his approval. "Very good! You are starting to understand Klingon ways. On a Klingon ship there is no such thing as a casual order. Every order is obeyed. If I say jump out an airlock, Pok will jump out an airlock."

Barclay nodded and Riker could see little beads of sweat breaking out on Barclay's forehead.

"Now," Gowron said, glancing at Captain Picard and smiling, then turning back to Barclay. "Attaining rank and positions on a Klingon ship will shock you. Do you know how it is done?"

Barclay changed the motion of his head from up and down to side to side, almost in one motion.

Gowron laughed. "Then listen and I will tell you."

* * *

"With the *Tagana* ready, the guards left the bridge, leaving only five Klingon warriors for the five stations. And young Pok. Three of my men, two of Qua'lon's men. An old Klingon, obviously trusted and protected by Qua'lon, stood at the operations station.

"Qugh, my operations officer, strode up behind the old Klingon.

"'I will take this station now,' he said, in the manner of the formal challenge of station.

"The old Klingon glanced at Qugh. 'Who are you that would take this station from me?'

"'Who are you that you would stop me?'

"The two growled at each other, then the old Klingon turned his back on Qugh and went to work at the station.

"Qugh grabbed the old man by the shoulder and spun him away, knocking him to the floor.

"The old Klingon warrior had great speed. He climbed back to his feet. Growled. He grabbed Qugh.

"The fight lasted only a moment. The old Klingon was no match for my officer. Again he found himself on his back on the floor.

"Qugh turned and began work at his new station.

"The old Klingon climbed to his feet, bowed to me, and took up a new position at the navigation console.

"I turned to Pok at that moment. 'Pok. *HighoS.*'

"Then I moved his attention from the fight to another matter. 'Do you wish to see your home one last time before you leave? Planet view!'

"A view of the planet Taganika quickly appeared on the main screen. I turned to Pok.

"He stared at it.

"'When I left my home,' I said, 'I was not much older than you. It was many years before I saw it again. When I did return it was as a warrior.'

"Then I turned to young warrior Pok. 'No one stands around on a Klingon ship. Everything must have a use. Even you, Pok. Choose your post.'

"I looked the young warrior right in the eye. 'But choose carefully. Remember what you have seen.'"

"Barclay!" Gowron said. "Pok must choose. Do so for him."

Riker saw that now Barclay really looked panicked. "I–I–I don't even know his choices. H–h–how can I choose?"

"Bah," Gowron said, waving his hand. "You are not listening. I told you there were five stations on the *Tagana.*"

"D–d–does Pok know any of the stations?" Barclay asked.

"Humans," Gowron said. He spit on the floor. "Bah. Think. As captain, I remove those who do not do their jobs. Otherwise, I told you how positions are chosen."

Riker could clearly see Barclay sweating now. And there was nothing Riker could do to help him. Doing so would bring the wrath of Gowron down on him, which was the last thing he wanted.

"I–I–I would chose to challenge the old Klingon."

Gowron stared at Barclay, his eyes blazing. "Why? Explain."

"B–B–Because Pok was young. He might be able to b–b–beat the old Klingon."

Gowron slapped his hand down hard on the table, causing Barclay to jump back and two of the guards to flinch. "Right," he said. "You can think, human."

Gowron took a deep drink of his blood wine, then held it up in the air. "Ferengi! More blood wine."

He looked at Barclay. "You could use some blood wine, also. You are thinking like a Klingon."

Barclay was not only thinking like a Klingon, he was sweating as if he was working out in a gym. But Riker could tell he was pleased with Gowron's praise. And having a Klingon tell a human he was thinking like a Klingon was high praise indeed.

Gowron glanced around the table, waiting for Quark to bring his wine. "If Pok had chosen any of my crew, they would have easily rebuffed him."

Admiral Jellico nodded. "Advancement is measured by physical skill, not proficiency at a task."

Gowron snorted. "Both, dear admiral. A warrior must be able to fight first. Then I, as strongest, judge his ability to perform the task." Gowron stared at Jellico. "Only the best at both rise to the top."

Quark broke the silence. "More wine." He banged the glass down in front of Gowron.

Riker had managed to keep his eyes focused on

Dax's hands on the table in front of her, away from Jellico's gaze. The last thing he needed to do was laugh at an insulted admiral, no matter how true the insult.

"Ah!" Gowron said after a long drink of wine. "Telling this story is thirsty work." He looked at the sweating Barclay. "And taking part also seems to be thirsty work. Ferengi! Bring him a wine."

Quark glanced at Barclay who looked pained, but said nothing.

"Now, back to Pok," Gowron said. "He must win a challenge."

"Pok moved to a position behind the old Klingon. He stood there, his young shoulders firm. His father would have been proud of him at that moment.

"'I will take this station, now,' he said.

"The old Klingon turned. 'Who challenges me for my station? Go away, little nothing.'

"The old Klingon turned his back on Pok. Pok grabbed the old warrior's shoulder and spun him around, tossing him to the floor. Again, the old Klingon surprised me by his speed. He attacked young Pok, but Torghn had taught the young warrior well. Pok soon beat the old warrior to the floor.

"This time the old warrior rose and left the bridge. He would find another station below.

"I gave Pok my approval. Then to my science officer I said, "Teach him the station. Teach him well.'"

* * *

Gowron took a long drink of blood wine, glared at Barclay for a moment, then went right back to telling his story.

"The next morning I sat in my command chair. Pok had done well, but the real first test of his navigation skills was at hand.

" 'Approaching the Balka System,' my communications officer said.

" 'Pok,' I said. 'Prepare for standard orbit.'

"Pok did as I ordered.

" 'Slow to impulse.'

"Again, Pok did as I had ordered. The ship slowed. The planet Balka appeared on the front screen. A brown, ugly-looking rock.

" 'Orbital track,' I ordered.

"Pok obeyed, taking the ship smoothly into orbit. I felt pride.

" 'Any other warships in the system?'

"My communications officer said, "Nothing in the system except a few cargo ships and a small runner vessel.'

" 'Good,' I said. 'Decloak. Drop shields and prepare to beam down to the surface.' I stood and moved toward the door. As I passed the navigation console I said, 'Pok. You are with me. These people trade in assassination. Death without honor. Stay close.'

"He followed my orders. He was at my side when we beamed into the bar.

"There are places in this sector of the galaxy that

are not fit for human, Klingon, or even Cardassians. The *BItuHpa* was such a place. Drugged smoke clogged the air. The smell of the unclean filled the room. Fifty varied species filled the room. No other Klingons. I could see Pok did not like the place.

"A Bolian singer worked a keyboard. Screeched out a tune. A large human bartender stared at us. He had two armed Bolian thugs at both doors. Possibly other hidden armaments. But I was not there for a fight.

"'There are no weapons allowed,' the bartender said, sneering at me. It was clear from his actions that he did not know who I was. Nor did he care.

"My guards and Pok closed in around me as the two thugs from the doors moved toward us.

"'No weapons!' I said. 'What kind of a *yInTagh* bar is this?'

"The bartender sneered at me. His yellowed teeth dripped saliva like a mad beast. 'I cater to a peace-loving clientele,' he said. He laughed. 'They don't like violence. If you really can't stand to part with your weapons, there are plenty of other bars in the city that will be happy to let you in armed. If *that's* what you looking for.'

"I growled at the two thugs, then turned back to the smiling bartender. 'You cannot expect us to give up our knives. We are Klingons.' I stepped closer to him, even though his breath repulsed me. 'I give you my word, no one will be harmed with them.'

"'The rule is no weapons,' the bartender said.

"I stepped closer again. 'I repeat. You cannot expect

us to give up our knives. We are Klingons. I have given my word.'

"The bartender thought for a moment. With what brain I do not know. Then he said, 'All right. But the disrupters have to go.'

"I glanced back at my guards and young Pok. Then I nodded and they all handed their disrupters to the two thugs.

"The bartender snorted at us and turned away.

"'These *nuchpu'* fear the very weapons they sell.' I turned to the guards. 'Mix yourself in among these people. See what you can overhear. And try not to kill anyone.'

"I moved to the bar. Pok stayed close, as I had ordered.

"'Do not be concerned, Pok,' I told the young warrior. 'Many things that do not look so, can become weapons.'

"The bartender moved down the bar toward us. His stench moved ahead of him. I had smelled better Caxtonian traders after long hauls.

"'Can I get you gentlemen something?' he said. Again he sneered and I hoped for the chance to remove that offending look from his face permanently. 'Or are you just here for the music?'

"'A drink,' I said. 'Pok. We should take the time to sample the local spirits.'

"I turned to the bartender. 'Necti. Pelet. Ora.'

"The bartender nodded and before a moment passed he had returned with three bottles. He sat them on the bar and pointed at each in turn. *'ngaSwI' wej. Hivje'mey.'*

"I looked at the ugly human bartender. 'You speak Klingon?'

"The bartender laughed, spraying us with his spit. 'I speak bartender.'

"Thankfully, he moved away."

Gowron took a deep drink of his blood wine and looked around the table. Riker could see that his audience was still with him.

"My voice needs a short rest," Gowron said. "My glass needs replenishing, too." He banged it on the table. "Ferengi! Another round for my listeners."

Then Gowron turned to Barclay and stared at him over the knife. "Do you follow the story?"

Barclay nodded yes.

"Good." Gowron sat back, smiling. "For soon Pok will be truly tested. His life for a right decision."

Riker could hear Barclay swallow. Even Captain Picard laughed with Gowron this time.

All Riker could think was, *Poor Mister Barclay.*

Chapter Ten

THE BRIDGE OF THE DURAS SISTERS' Bird of Prey was dark under cloak. Lursa held her position in the command chair while B'Etor paced to her left. Only the click and hum of the ship broke the silence.

On the main screen the Federation *Deep Space Nine* station floated against the field of black stars. The Federation flagship *Enterprise* held position near it, seeming to dominate all around it. Gowron's ship and a second Klingon Bird of Prey held an area of space on the opposite side of the station.

The surprise had been the two Cardassian ships.

Lursa had not expected Cardassians.

B'Etor stopped beside her sister. "I have no patience for this." Her voice was low and firm.

"I know, sister." Lursa said. "But we must wait. Hoq is on the station now. He will contact dRacLa.

We will learn Gowron's movements. Until then we wait."

"This could take days."

"It might." Lursa remained staring at the two Cardassian ships holding off the station. For some reason their presence bothered her. She was willing to face the station. The *Enterprise*. Gowron's ships. But Cardassians she did not expect.

But now all they could do was wait, holding at long-range scan distance, until their operatives gave them more information. They had no other choice.

Again B'Etor stopped her pacing and said, "I hate waiting."

And again Lursa said, "I know, sister."

Riker watched as Gowron glanced around at his audience. The Klingon was a good storyteller. There was no doubt of that. He even had Admiral Jellico interested, which was more than the admiral seemed to be during the official meetings.

"Do any of you know the drinks I talked of?" Gowron asked. "Pelat? Ora? Necti?"

Riker nodded. "I have tasted Pelat. Sweet, made from a fermented Talaran berry, if I remember right."

"You remember right," Gowron said. Then he smiled as mischievous a smile as Riker had ever seen. "Commander. You know your drinks, I see."

Riker smiled back at him, toasting him with a glass of blood wine. "I know how. And have had much practice."

Gowron laughed and toasted Riker in return. "Do you know of the others?"

"No," Riker said. The word *Necti* sounded familiar, but more as a poison than a drink.

Gowron nodded. "I am not surprised. Ora has little kick. A nasty taste. Not much worth the effort. But one of my guards drank it, so I ordered it. Necti is another matter. I drink it at times. A Birani beverage. They say it is made from reactant fluid distilled in the blood of Necti warriors."

Gowron glanced at Admiral Jellico's shocked look, but made no comment. "If I had a bottle of it here, I would let you smell it. Like fresh ground turned for a grave."

Gowron looked at Riker, who was nodding. He had remembered correctly. "Necti is a poison to humans."

"Correct, Commander," Gowron said. "To *all* of the more delicate species. Ferengi. Romulan. Human. To a Klingon it burns going down, and sears the stomach as well as the brain. I have known of Klingons who have died drinking it too fast."

Gowron smiled. "It is an interesting drink. And plays a part in Pok's story."

"I could tell young Pok enjoyed his Pelat. I sipped at the Necti. Its burn filled me while my guards mingled among the crowd. The singer finished her song and I yelled across the bar to her. 'You sing well.'

"'Thank you,' she called back. 'Requests?'

"'Klingon opera?' I did not expect her to know any.

She appeared to be human. But she surprised me. Without looking away from me she started into *tlhIngan jIH,* a popular opera about the nature of being Klingon.

"Pok and I sat and enjoyed it. She finished and we cheered her, as did my guards. The rest of the bar joined in.

"I moved from my place at the bar, taking my drink. Pok stayed at my side.

"'Few humans understand the spirit of Klingon opera,' I told her. 'You are a true artist.'

"She smiled at me. 'The melodies are simple. Quite repetitive. The difficulty is handling the tonality.'

"She brushed against my leg and I responded back to her in a gentle manner, leading her on as I have seen humans do to their women.

"'The trick is,' she said, 'you must be harsh with it.'

"'You understand Klingons well. Sing it again.'

"Others close by in the bar agreed.

"Again she sang the Klingon opera *tlhIngan jIH.*

"Again we cheered her performance.

"'We must show our appreciation,' I said loudly to Pok.

"'Really,' she said. 'That won't be necessary.' She knew what I intended. But she had pleased me. It was Klingon custom.

"I turned to Pok. 'Choose,' I told him."

Gowron smiled at Barclay who again looked startled at the sudden turn in the story. "Do you not understand?"

Barclay swallowed. "I–I–I do not, sir."

Riker felt almost sorry for Barclay this time. Gowron was asking him to fulfill a very little-known Klingon custom of showing appreciation for a performance. "Lieutenant," Riker said, leaning toward Barclay while smiling at Gowron. "Klingons show their appreciation of good art or performance by smashing something. Then paying for it. Sort of tipping, with an act in the middle."

Gowron continued to stare at Barclay as he first looked at Riker, then back at the Klingon leader.

"Choose," Gowron said. "Action. The song was good. What would Pok choose?"

"A bar g–g–glass," Barclay said.

"Bah," Gowron said. "I must not have described fully. The song, the opera by this human woman singer was superb. A bar glass costs nothing. Breaking it would have been an insult to her."

"A ch–chair?" Barclay asked. Again he was sweating.

"Better," Gowron said. "Much better. What Pok actually chose."

"Pok pointed to the singer's chair. My guard took it. Smashed it into small pieces. The crowd yelled its approval.

"I turned to the singer. 'It is done. We pay for what we destroy.' I offered her a bar of latinum.

"'Latinum?' She stared at the bar. Did not take it.

"'If it is not acceptable to you,' I said. I moved to put the bar back into my pocket.

" 'No. No. It is acceptable.' She almost ripped the bar from my hand. Then she turned it over, checking its weight and value.

" 'Not enough?' I asked. I knew it was far more than the value of her simple chair.

" 'More than enough,' she said. Then she looked me in the eye. 'Is there something more you wanted?'

" 'Information.'

" 'I thought Klingons took information,' she said. 'I was not aware that they paid for it.'

"I stepped right up and looked into her face, sneering at her. 'The latinum is for the chair. The information you will give for free.' She did not back away, but I saw the flicker of fear cross her eyes. I knew I had her at that moment.

" 'I am looking for a weapons dealer. One who could get me something. Something like this.' I pulled out the Romulan assassins probe that killed my friend.

"She recognized it for what it was. She became nervous. She stepped away from me. 'I wouldn't know anything about that. I only sing here.'

"I stepped back up to her face. 'You are not blind. You see who makes the deals. Who sets up the meetings.'

"The singer moved another step away from me, shaking her head. I took her by the arm, gripping her hard.

"Behind me, the bartender shouted, 'Stop him!'

"I turned her around so that I could see my two guards and Pok make very short work of the two thugs. I do not think any of my men even took a blow. I know young Pok did not.

"The crowd in the bar seemed frozen. Silence filled the place. I turned back to the singer. 'Now,' I said, growling in her face. 'Whom do they come to see?'

"Many a Klingon warrior had backed down to my threats. She was no exception. She pointed to the bartender. 'Meska. He's the one who arranges it all.'

"I tossed the singer aside, being careful not to hurt her seriously. A good singer of Klingon opera must always be given appreciation. I moved to the bartender. He moved to get away, but I easily stopped him.

"'You have information?' I said.

"'You see,' he said. 'This is why we don't allow weapons in here. I should have never let you keep your knives.'

"'My guards did not use their knives,' I told him. 'I have kept my word. But as I told my young comrade, there are always weapons.'

"Holding the bartender with one hand, I picked up the glass of Necti. I held it in front of the bartender's wide eyes. 'How often do you serve Necti, bartender? Have you ever tried it?'

"I moved to feed the bartender a sip of Necti. He locked his mouth shut. Wouldn't drink. I was not surprised.

"'No?' I said, pulling the glass away from his face. 'Then tell me what I want to know.'

"He did not answer, so I tried again to give him just a sip. He did not let me.

"'Who brings the probes into this sector?'

"The bartender shook his head. 'I don't know. I don't.'

"I did not believe him. I held the glass above his face and splashed a little of the drink in his eyes.

"He screamed. Then he called out, 'My eyes! I can't see. My eyes!'

"I lifted him into the air. 'Tell me now, bartender, before I pour the whole bottle on you.'

"'Shipments of weapons come through here all the time,' he said quickly. I lowered him back to the floor. His hands worked at his eyes.

"'More,' I said.

"He shook his head. 'I don't ask what they carry.'

"'This shipment would have come from the Soltaris System.'

"The bartender tried to twist out of my grasp, but I held on and poured the rest of the glass on him

"Again he screamed.

"'What ship?'

"Trying to rub the liquid off his face, he said, 'The *Toofa*. A Pakled vessel.'

"I was disgusted. I hated Pakleds. They were stupid beasts. "'When?'

"'Sixteen hours,' he said. 'It left here sixteen hours ago headed back to Soltaris.'

"I continued to hold the bartender by the shirt. 'T'Rok!' I called out to my guard. 'We return to the ship. Pok! The Necti.'

"Pok did as I ordered and handed me the half-empty bottle of Necti.

"The bartender kept saying, 'No. No. No.' Over

and over. I held the bottle up for a moment, then tipped it up and drank the rest of it.

"I let the bartender go and threw the bottle against the back wall. 'No sense in wasting it, eh?'

"I stepped to a position in front of Pok and my two guards. With a nod to the singer, I said, 'Now.' And we returned to the ship. But now we had a lead.

Riker watched as Gowron rolled his empty glass across the table, then shouted "Ferengi! Wine!"

He looked at Barclay with a cold smile. "The Ferengi does not know how to keep his customers happy. Maybe I should give him a taste of Necti? What do you think, Barclay?"

At the shocked look in Barclay's eyes, Gowron sat back and laughed.

Chapter Eleven

NIBO HOQ GLANCED in both directions down the seemingly empty corridor, then moved quickly along the row of doors. His thin frame and flowing green robe were in stark contrast to the dull, heavy feeling of the corridor. This area was part of the station's guest quarters and seemed to be empty. And he moved without a sound.

He'd booked a room for three nights in a similar section of the station, giving the excuse to those in Ops that his ship needed slight repairs before he could go on. Since he was a Saurian merchant who had been on the station numbers of times before, he was not questioned, even with the Klingon/Federation meetings going on.

He glanced around. His room was not in this area of the station, but if stopped, he would claim he had simply gotten lost while looking for his own room. This area of the station did look almost the same as the area of his room. So far he had only seen two guards and they had not stopped him.

Hoq kept moving, searching for the door with the special mark. He had something to deliver. Nibo Hoq dealt in much more than just the goods that filled his cargo hold. His most profitable item had always been information and he was very good at getting it. And getting paid highly for selling it.

A faint gray mark caught his eye. Nothing more than a scratch with a hooked end near the upper corner of the door. Yet he knew instantly it was the signal he was looking for.

Glancing in both directions, he moved three doors farther down the hall from the mark, then knocked lightly. He was very careful to stay away from the call button on the door.

He could hear a rustle faintly behind the door, then the door was pushed open by hand, by a large Klingon warrior. It did not automatically open, otherwise movement would have shown up in the station's security monitors.

Hoq nodded and slipped into the dark room while the Klingon pushed the door closed. Only a single candle burned in the center of the spartan room. A thin mat had been laid out on the floor in one corner. No other signs of life, even though Hoq suspected the Klingon had been in the room for most of four days.

"You have information?" the Klingon said, moving over and standing across the candle from Hoq. His hard features and ridge lines in his face cast dark shadows on his forehead.

"I have what you and your friends seek," Nibo Hoq said. "Do you have my price?"

The Klingon snorted, then reached into his vest and pulled out a packet. He tossed it at Hoq, who caught it easily. Hoq unwrapped it, checking the amount. It was what he had asked from Lursa. More than enough to make the trip profitable.

He put the package inside his cape and looked the Klingon directly in the eye. "Gowron beams back to his ship immediately after the meetings break up, in late afternoon. Then he comes back and drinks in Quark's until fairly late, telling stories. He is there now, as we speak."

The Klingon laughed. "He always believed stories were important. I see he has not changed."

Hoq nodded, but said nothing.

"Go on," the Klingon said.

"He is officially a Federation guest," Hoq said. "He is guarded well, by both his men and the Federation. When the station's shields drop, after the meetings, he is the first to beam to his ship."

The Klingon glowered at Hoq for a short time in the flickering candlelight, then suddenly smiled. "I understand."

Hoq bowed and moved back toward the door. "I did not expect to have to explain my information. Now, I am needed at my ship." He indicated the door and that the Klingon should open it for him.

The Klingon moved to a position in front of the door, then turned to Hoq. "How do I know you will not sell your information about me."

Hoq laughed. "One buyer per trip. It is a rule that I find helps keep me out of trouble. And keeps my buyers returning for my services."

The Klingon nodded and turned back to face the door, as if he were about to open it. Instead he pulled out his knife, and with a quick turn, buried it into Hoq's stomach.

Nibo Hoq felt the suddenness of the thrust and the sudden loss of air from his lungs.

He tried to pull away, but the Klingon held him close until Hoq could feel the strength in his legs draining with his blood down his front.

He fought, but against the strength of the Klingon it did no good.

Finally he stopped struggling.

He knew he was going to die.

He looked into the cold black eyes of the Klingon. "You did not need to do this."

The Klingon yanked the knife out and let Hoq fall to the floor. "Information is a two-edged blade," the Klingon said, standing over him. "I have no desire to be cut."

"You had my word," Nibo Hoq said, the sentence bubbling in his throat as blood filled his lungs.

"Your word," the Klingon said.

The last thing Nibo Hoq ever heard was the Klingon laughing.

* * *

Gowron waited until all his audience's drinks were refilled. Riker was startled to find that this evening he had finished one full glass of blood wine. Gowron had insisted that Quark bring him another, and secretly, Riker was glad he did. Dax touched his hand and indicated the empty glass with a smile. She was half laughing at him. He enjoyed that.

Riker leaned over and whispered in her ear. "Gowron's stories make me thirsty."

She laughed out loud but said nothing, because Gowron was about to start. But to Riker her laugh promised good moments together ahead. He just hoped the situation would allow them the moments. They were both Starfleet officers. Time had a way of disappearing for them.

Gowron finished a long drink of blood wine, sighed heavily, and then with only a quick glance at the sweating Lieutenant Barclay, started back into his story.

"I assumed it would not take our ship long to overtake the Pakled ship. They are slow slugs at best. I was right.

"'Picking up a vessel within scanning range,' my communications officer, ChaqI, said, only three hours after we had left the bar.

"'The Pakled ship?' I asked, spinning in my command chair so that I could address ChaqI directly.

"'Yes.'

"'Cloak the ship.'

"'Cloaking the ship,' ChaqI said.

"The lights dimmed. We were cloaked.

"'The cargo hold is empty,' ChaqI said. 'Ten humanoids, all Pakled.'

"'Let me see this Pakled ship,' I ordered. I turned back to the main screen. The ship appeared on the screen.

"'They are slowing,' ChaqI said.

"'*qoH!*' I was not happy. 'You did not engage the cloaking device fast enough. They have detected us.'

"'No, *DevwI!*' ChaqI said. 'They have a coolant leak. If they do not power down, the warp engines will overheat.'

"Laughter broke over the bridge. I, too, laughed.

"'*HuH* Pakled,' ChaqI said. 'They do not fix their vessels. They do not even understand how. A ship must be treated with honor. They treat theirs as so much garbage. How can they do this?'

"'They are Pakled,' I said. It was enough to explain.

"'They go to impulse,' ChaqI said.

"'Pok,' I ordered. 'Go to number two tactical station.' Then I turned to face Surgh, my best navigator. He had stepped into Pok's position. 'Bring us out of warp! I want to be right in the Pakled's face when we engage the tractor beam.'

"Surgh did as I told him. The viewscreen in front of me changed to show the Pakled ship. It was an ugly thing. More like a Ferengi cargo ship than anything else.

"'We will make these Pakled tell us,' I said, 'who purchased the Romulan hunter killer probe. But they must be questioned with care. Frighten a Pakled too much and I will never get the information. At least not information that will be of any use to us.'

" 'Dead stop,' Surgh said.

" 'Raise shields! Decloak. Pull them in with the tractor beam. I want us close, as close as we can get.'

"My orders were followed, and the Pakled ship was drawn in close to the *Tagana*.

" 'We are being hailed,' ChaqI said.

" 'Not a surprise,' I said. 'On screen.'

"The Pakled captain appeared on-screen. He had a round face, small black eyes sunk in his pink flesh. His nose looked as if a warrior had pounded it flat with a fist. Sweat seemed to coat his pale skin like a sickness. He was frightened and very nervous, as I had planned.

" 'We do nothing wrong,' the captain said. His voice almost squeaked, like a comm system gone bad. I always hated Pakled voices. This captain's voice was no exception.

" 'We are Pakled,' the captain went on. 'We are honest traders. Why do you hold us here?'

" 'We need information,' I said.

" 'I don't know anything,' the captain said.

" 'No Pakled knows anything,' ChaqI said behind me.

" *'yltamchoH,'* I said to ChaqI. Then I lowered my voice to the Pakled captain. 'You are Pakled.'

" 'Yes. We are Pakled,' the captain repeated.

" 'Then you have knowledge. You are not stupid.'

" 'No. We are not stupid.'

" 'Then you will beam over and tell us what we need to know,' I said.

" 'No!' The Pakled captain said. 'I am afraid. I will not beam over.'

" 'Why?'

" 'You are Klingon. We are Pakled.'

" 'I do not understand you, Pakled.'

"The captain nodded. 'It is difficult to understand.' He looked very seriously at me. I managed not to laugh.

" 'Then,' I said, very seriously, 'you must come aboard our ship and explain why you are afraid to come aboard.'

"The round-faced Captain nodded. 'Yes. I will do that. I will beam over and explain.'

" 'You are a good negotiator, captain,' I said. Again I managed to keep my smile hidden. But that was not an easy task.

"The Pakled captain beamed a huge smile, showing me his stubby little teeth. 'Yes. We are Pakled.'

"I turned to Surgh. 'Go to the transporter room. Beam him here. Pok, take the navigation station.'

"I waited until Pok was in position, then said, 'Lower shields and release the tractor beam.' "

Gowron stared at Admiral Jellico. "Admiral, you suggested yesterday that my crew is not trained to do a job. Only to fight."

"Well, I—" Admiral Jellico tried to object, but Gowron waived away the obviously unprepared admiral's answer and turned to Barclay.

"Barclay," Gowron said. "Do you know how to run a tactical station on a Klingon Bird of Prey?"

Riker watched as Barclay shook his head quickly. "N–no, sir."

"So, if Pok did not know the difference between a tractor beam and a cloaking device? What would happen?"

Barclay again shook his head.

Gowron snarled at Barclay. Then he said, "The ship would cloak. And then scare the Pakled captain. Right?"

This time, Barclay nodded yes.

"And a scared, stupid Pakled would try to get away. With a broken warp coil. Their ship would explode. We would get no information."

"I–I–I can s–s–see that, sir."

"Good," Gowron said.

"If Pok did not know the difference between shields and firing disrupters?"

"He would destroy the P–p–pakled ship."

"Correct. If tractor beam was still engaged and he fired the disrupters?" Gowron stared at Barclay, clearly waiting for an answer. Riker knew the answer. And he knew Barclay did, too.

"S–s–sir," Barclay said. "That would create a feed-back loop that would destroy your sh–ship."

Gowron smiled at Captain Picard. "Captain. You train your crew well."

"Thank you," Picard said, tipping his glass in a half-toast. "I am honored at the compliment."

Gowron turned to Admiral Jellico. "If Pok was not

trained as well, would I risk my life? The life of my ship? Giving him a post such as I did?"

Admiral Jellico swallowed hard. "Obviously not."

Gowron nodded. The admiral's answer was enough, it seemed, for Gowron. Riker had really enjoyed watching Gowron take apart the admiral that way. He wasn't sure it would help the last days of the meetings, but it couldn't hurt at this point.

Gowron sat back, smiling. "My story continues with yet another twist."

"Pok correctly dropped the shields and released the tractor beam, as I had ordered. The Pakled captain beamed onto the bridge and three of my men surrounded him.

"'Shields up!' I ordered Pok.

"He again followed my command.

"'Why did you do that?' the round Pakled captain asked. Up close I could smell his sour odor. Like fruit left too long in the hot sun. To my nose, it was not a pleasant smell.

"'To frighten you, Captain,' I said. 'Is it working?'

"'I am Pakled,' the stupid oaf said.

"I laughed. 'So you keep telling us. Tell us one thing more, Pakled. Tell us who purchased your last shipment of weapons from the Soltaris System.'

"'Who told you that?' the Pakled captain asked. His little eyes shifted around, back and forth, as he stared up at my men surrounding him.

"'A friend of yours,' I said, leaning in close. 'Meska. A bartender on Balka.'

" 'Yes. He's the one. We sell him many weapons.' The round fool puffed up like a blowfish. Proud. 'Contraband. Illegal.'

" 'The bartender,' I said. *'QI'yah.* Are you sure, Pakled?'

"Yes. He is the one. He purchases much. I sell him everything. You want something? I can get it.'

"I turned and went back to my command chair. 'Get this *veQ* off my bridge.' I dropped into my chair. 'Set a course back to the Balka System. Warp nine. We will teach this bartender that Klingons do not like being played with.' "

Riker watched as Gowron paused, then glanced at Captain Picard. "It is getting late."

The captain nodded. "Yes, but you tell an interesting story."

Gowron smiled. "You honor me." Gowron turned to Barclay. "Do you wish to continue?"

"Y–yes, sir."

Gowron turned to the admiral. "And you, Admiral."

"Captain Picard is right," Admiral Jellico said. "You tell a good story. Is this a good place to break until tomorrow evening? Or is there a better one?"

Gowron smiled at the admiral. "A politician. There is a better breaking place not far ahead."

"Then please do continue," the admiral said.

Gowron downed the last of his blood wine and leaned forward to continue telling his story.

* * *

"It would take us over an hour to return to the Balka System. I was hungry. I knew young Pok must be also. So I ordered him to go with me to the mess hall. To continue his lessons.

"The hall was empty for the moment, but there was still food in the center of the mess table. We loaded our plates and sat.

"'When we catch this *veQ* of a bartender,' I said to Pok, 'I will let you have the honor of killing him. But a warrior must know more than just how to kill an enemy. You must know why you fight. Your history. Do you know your family line?'

"Pok's mouth was full of food. He nodded.

"'Good,' I said. 'When you die with honor, you will serve with all your warrior ancestors in the Black Fleet. And you must know to greet them all by name.'

"At that moment the old Klingon warrior loyal to Qua'lon arrived in the mess. He took a plate of food, and even though the hall was empty except for us, he sat next to Pok.

"I whispered across to Pok. 'You must finish this now, Pok. Establish between you who is superior.'

"The old Klingon was eating, pretending to ignore Pok. Pok reached over and took the old Klingon's plate of food.

"The old Klingon stared at Pok, then growled. He got up and left the room. Without challenging Pok.

"'It is over between you,' I told the young warrior. 'He will not challenge you again. But do not dismiss his whole life because of this. Old warriors once were young. The honors they have gathered should not fade with time.'

"I made Pok look me straight in the eye. 'Understand this, Pok,' I said. 'He is no longer your enemy. Make him your friend. Show him you honor his past.'

"At that moment the comm demanded my attention. 'Sir,' Surgh's voice came strong into the mess hall. 'We are approaching Balka.'

"'Good,' I said, standing. 'We will repay this bartender, who sent us chasing wild *Ooghmey*.'

"We transported directly back into the bar, this time with our disrupters drawn and ready. I took with us the old Klingon warrior and my two guards, T'lak and Ler'at. Both had been with me for years. Both were with me when Torghn was killed.

"The singer was doing her job, but stopped after she noticed us. The bar seemed much emptier. The bartender and his two thugs were gone.

"I moved to the singer. 'Where is he?'

"'You are too late,' she said. 'He is gone.'

"'Where?'

"She shook her head. 'I wish I knew.'

"*'QI'yah'*

"'If you catch him,' the singer said, 'kill him slowly for me. He owes me three weeks pay, and the tips in this place aren't enough to keep a wheeze beetle alive.'

"The singer slammed her fist on the piano. I was shocked at her anger. It was real. I knew that for certain.

"'If he were here now,' she said, 'I would personally rip his heart out.'

"'I would help you,' I said. 'Who would know where he has gone?'

"She shrugged. 'Some of his connections. Maybe. But they don't come in here often. Only when they need something.'

"I pulled up a chair and sat down, indicating that Pok do the same. 'Then we will wait.'

"The singer smiled at me. 'Then I will sing for you. But you will leave your disrupters.'

"I glanced around at the bar patrons but saw no one who would be of danger to us. So I gave my guards and Pok the signal to place our weapons with the person filling in as bartender. He looked so relieved, I laughed at him. He then served us our drinks on the house.

"Pok and I sat at one table. My two guards and the old Klingon sat at another table. We listened to the singer do a Klingon opera. Again, she was good to listen to.

"As she sang her song, I turned and whispered to Pok. 'Meska the bartender was only a buyer for the real assassins. I suspect someone among my own people to be one of them. How else would the probe have found its way into my own belongings?'

"I stared at young Pok. 'Tell me. Whom do you suspect?'"

Gowron stared at Lieutenant Barclay so hard Riker started to feel uneasy just sitting beside him. Finally Barclay said, "S–sir? I don't unders–s–stand."

"Whom do you suspect?" Gowron said. "You are

playing the role of young Pok. Do you not think I took the three warriors with us to the surface for a reason?"

"You s–s–suspect all three?"

Gowron roared his laughter. "Of course not. The old Klingon I knew to be an honorable warrior. He could have left service to live a comfortable life long before. But he stayed on, leaving himself open to challenges by younger warriors. Warriors like Pok. Do not think that because a warrior is old, he is any less than he was."

"I–I meant no disrespect, sir."

Gowron waved the comment away. "I will answer for you, even though the clues have been throughout the story. It is getting late. T'lak had made me uncomfortable of late. His actions were odd. I had suspected him."

"How did you catch him?" Riker asked. He surprised himself by his sudden question. Dax smiled at him again.

"I will tell you," Gowron said. "And then the evening will be at an end."

"The singer had finished her song and the bar applauded. I shouted to her. 'Well sung, again.'

"She stood and held out her hand. 'Why don't you just give me the money this time. I promise I will break something later of equivalent value.'

"I laughed at her joke. I turned to T'lak. 'I am short of money. Give this woman something and I shall repay it twice when we return to the ship.'

"T'lak reached into his pocket and pulled out

something he kept in his fist. He stood and moved toward the singer. But I stopped him before he handed her what he carried. I grabbed his hand and forced it over and open.

"He held two Acta crystals. Two very distinct Acta crystals. Crystals I had marked earlier with special marks. And given to Meska the bartender in payment for the drinks.

"'Acta crystals are rare in this sector,' I said to T'lak. 'Just earlier today I had some. They passed from my hand to Meska the bartender's. Now they have somehow made their way into yours. How can that be?'

"I twisted and shoved T'lak hard. He fell to the floor and the old Klingon, Pok, and my other guard pulled him to his feet and held him.

"'It was you, T'lak. You betrayed me.'

"I turned my back on him.

"Then I said, not looking at him, 'Now, you will tell me everything. I want to know where that bartender went. Tell me now before I kill you.'

"My back was turned, but suddenly I heard a scuffle. Then a disrupter went off. I turned quickly, but not quickly enough. The singer had killed T'lak. I was about to turn on her when I noticed T'lak had a small disrupter in his hand. He must have kept it hidden on him and pulled it.

"'He got away,' the old Klingon said. 'He was about to kill you. She shot him.'

"I turned to her. Nodded my thanks. 'I thought weapons were not allowed.'

111

" 'That rule is for customers only,' she said. And then she smiled at me. I knew at that moment she had been telling the truth about the bartender.

"I turned back to my men. 'Search him.'

"They searched T'lak's body until they found a credit slip. The old Klingon handed it to me. I studied it, then handed it to the singer. 'You recognize this?'

" 'A Galorine credit slip," she said. She handed it back to me. 'Meska had dealings on Galor. Connections. He might have gone there.'

" 'Galor?' I did not know of such a place. 'Do you know where it is?'

"The singer brightened at my lack of knowledge. 'Take me with you. I will show you. Get me off this forsaken hole of a planet.'

"I did not like the idea. She could tell.

" 'I will not get in the way,' she said.

"I did owe her my life. This seemed to be the right thing. 'See that you do not,' I said. 'Come then. To Galor.'

"We left T'lak on the floor. He died without honor."

Gowron stood. "The hour is late. The morning is not far. I depart."

With that, almost before the rest of them could get to their feet, he headed across the now far less-crowded bar and out onto the Promenade.

Barclay looked vastly relieved. Riker patted him on the back. "You're doing fine."

Barclay only nodded his thanks and followed Picard and the admiral toward the entrance. Riker turned to Dax. "Another try at dinner tomorrow night?"

She smiled. "I'd love that. After the meeting?"

"Perfect," Riker said.

She walked beside him, silently, until they reached Ops. Then with a slight wave from her he transported with Captain Picard back to the *Enterprise.*

And to what he hoped would be a good night's sleep.

Chapter Twelve

"Picard to Riker."

The call woke Riker.

"Go ahead," Riker said to the darkness over his bed. He pushed himself up and glanced at the clock near his bed. It had only been four hours since he had fallen asleep. He still had three hours before the day's meetings were to start.

"I need you to meet me in transporter room one in fifteen minutes."

"Yes, sir," Riker said.

Without a wasted motion he was out of bed and getting ready. Twelve minutes later he walked into the transporter room. Captain Picard was already there.

"Sorry to wake you, Number One," he said as he stepped up on the pad.

"Not a problem," Riker said. "Troubles, I gather."

"I think so," Picard said. Then he said to the transporter chief, "Energize."

The next moment they were being greeted in Ops by Commander Sisko and Dax.

"This looks serious," Riker said softly to Dax as they headed for the lift.

"It is," she said.

Within a few minutes they met Odo in a corridor that Riker figured to be an empty living or guest quarters. But he wasn't familiar enough with the layout of the station to be sure.

"Any more information?" Sisko asked Odo as they stopped in front of an open door.

"No, sir," Odo said. "We have left everything as we found it." He indicated they all should enter.

Just inside the door was the body of a Saurian, his long, slender fingers and thin frame looking even thinner in death. His blood had pooled under him, leaving a damp, almost metallic smell in the air. His eyes were open, staring. Obviously his last sight had been his attacker.

Riker stepped inside the door and around the body to give room for Picard and Sisko to follow.

"Knife wound, into the lungs," Odo said, kneeling over the body and pointing to the chest. "His name is Nibo Hoq. He is a Saurian trader, with a ship full of legal goods. He has been here three days for repairs."

Picard knelt over the Saurian and studied him for a moment, then stood. "Any other record?"

Odo nodded. "He had a reputation of being able to

deliver information to the highest bidder. He was never caught doing anything illegal, but we suspected him and had kept him under fairly tight watch."

"Nothing, I gather, came up?" Picard asked.

"Correct, sir," Odo said. "Nibo Hoq did nothing suspicious during his three days here."

"Except die," Dax said.

"Except that," Odo agreed.

Riker glanced around the empty room. At first glance there was no sign that anyone had inhabited the room since the last cleaning. But then on closer inspection he could see smudges on the table. And in the center of the floor what looked to be a few small drops of something. He moved over to them and knelt, trying to get a better picture of just what they were.

"Wax," Odo said, moving over and standing above Riker. "From first guess I would say simple candle wax." He turned and pointed to the door. "Sensors in the door were circumvented so that it could be pushed open and closed without station monitors catching the movement."

"Is that easy to do?" Picard asked.

Commander Sisko laughed without humor. "Cardassian technology has many different ways in and around it. This was a new one for us."

"So how did you find him in here?" Picard asked, pointing to the Saurian. "He doesn't appear to have been dead that long."

"I would estimate two hours at most," Odo said.

"Does this have anything to do with the meetings?" Riker asked. "Or the bombing?"

Commander Sisko motioned to Odo that he would explain the rest. "That's where the main problem comes in," Sisko said. "A guard noticed the door slightly ajar. When he pushed it open to investigate, he was hit and knocked out. He said the Saurian was already dead. He saw that as he opened the door. He also said it was a Klingon warrior who hit him."

"What?" Riker asked.

"He is certain?" Picard asked.

"Yes, Captain," Odo said. "The guard can't identify his attacker, but he knows it was a Klingon."

Picard glanced at Riker who only shook his head. Riker didn't want to fully believe what he had just heard. The implications of that would take a moment to sink in. He went back to studying the room to give his mind some time to work. He could see no other evidence. And nothing that would make any sense of this so far.

"So how many Klingons are on the station at this moment?" Picard asked, after a moment of silence in the room.

"None," Commander Sisko said.

"That we know of," Odo said. "All the Klingons with Gowron's ships beam back to their respective ships every night. There are no others here."

"And one could not remain behind," Dax said. "We have a careful check system, as well as transporter records. No one stayed behind after Quark's closed last night. We have already double-checked."

"Shields have been kept up except during beaming," Sisko said. "And we have monitored every single transmission to or from the station."

Picard glanced down at the body of the Saurian. "Yet a Klingon was seen here?"

Sisko nodded.

"It seems," Picard said, "that we have what they used to call a locked-room mystery in detective fiction. A Klingon is the prime suspect. Yet no Klingon could have done this."

Riker moved back to the door and studied the lock and the door. Then he tried to push it closed. It was very heavy. And very hard to push. He doubted the thin, light Saurian could have done it. But a Klingon warrior could easily have.

"What information would have been valuable to a Klingon?" Picard asked. He glanced around the room, looking for any answer. "Information that this Saurian might have?"

"Valuable enough to kill for?" Dax said. "I don't know."

"A threat against Gowron's life?" Riker said. "It fits with the Cardassian warnings."

"That it does, Number One," Picard said. "But just how?"

"I don't know how," Odo said. "But at the moment I have two bodies, a rogue Klingon, and no answers. I don't like that."

"Neither do I," Commander Sisko said, his deep voice filling the small room. "Neither do I."

On that point, Riker had to agree. He didn't like it either. And he had a very bad feeling about all this.

Lursa sat in the command chair in the near darkness of the Bird of Prey bridge. She kept staring at the Federation station on long-range scan. She grew tired of waiting. They had waited for over a day now. Cloaked. Sitting in the darkness. The day's meetings between the Federation and the dog Gowron were about to start. She had heard nothing from her contacts.

Behind her the door to bridge hissed open. A moment later B'Etor stood by her side. She said nothing. There was nothing to say.

"Take the watch," Lursa said. "I will get food."

She stood. B'Etor slipped into the command chair.

They could not afford to wait much longer. Yet they had no choice.

She was almost off the bridge when her communications officer said, "Incoming message from the station. Cloaked channel."

Instantly B'Etor was beside Lursa behind the officer. He worked quickly to decode the message, then turned to them. "Gowron is always the first to beam off the station after the day's meetings."

"Anything more?"

"No."

B'Etor turned, almost angry. "What is dRacLa thinking? His information is worthless."

"No, sister," Lursa said. "It is good information.

Exact information. And it will allow us to carry on with our plan."

B'Etor stopped and turned. Ready to argue with her sister. But when she saw Lursa was smiling, she stopped. Lursa had not smiled in days. And only the possibility of Gowron's death would make her smile so. This message truly was good.

Chapter Thirteen

THE MORNING SESSION of the meetings again gained no
ground. Picard felt more frustrated than ever. With
little sleep, the two deaths, and Admiral Jellico's
stubborn refusal to compromise with Gowron, Picard
felt totally at a loss for a solution. The only place the
parties seemed to be getting along was during
Gowron's story sessions. They were certainly far
more interesting than the meetings.

As the parties around the table stood for their lunch
break, Picard turned to Gowron. "I am very much
enjoying your story of young Pok."

"Thank you, Captain," Gowron said. "I enjoy
telling it."

"Will you have time to finish the story this evening?
It will be our last evening together."

Gowron nodded, thinking. "There is still much to tell."

Gowron glanced up at Picard, and instantly Picard knew Gowron had caught on to Picard's idea. Maybe a session of the story at lunch would help break down some of the barriers.

Also, Picard had the feeling that if anything was going to come of these meetings, Gowron was setting up the possibility in the telling of his story.

"If my listeners are interested," Gowron said to the room. "I could continue the story of Pok for a short time during lunch. Tonight the end will be reached without strain."

"A wonderful idea," Picard said, loudly. He turned to Jellico. "Admiral?"

The admiral hesitated for a moment, then nodded. "I would enjoy that."

"Good," Picard said. He turned to Riker. "Number One, have Lieutenant Barclay meet us in Quark's in five minutes."

"Yes, sir," Riker said. And as he turned away Picard caught Riker's smile.

Picard noted that it didn't take long for Gowron's audience to be settled around the same table in the back of Quark's bar. Two Federation security officers and two Klingon guards stood watch over the group a short distance away.

Dax sat next to Riker again. They seemed to be sharing a great deal of time and laughter lately. Picard noted that they made a good couple.

122

Lieutenant Barclay was the last to arrive by only a minute. He got settled as Quark and Rom both scurried around serving drinks and everyone's order for lunch.

Picard had ordered only a small salad. Riker and Dax both ordered sandwiches. Jellico had a bowl of soup with extra crackers. And Gowron a bowl of *gagh*. As he claimed when it was placed in front of him, it was his favorite food.

Gowron took a few bites and washed it down with a large drink of ale. He then looked around at his audience and without a second's hesitation started into his story.

"We took the woman singer with us out of the bar. I felt she could be trusted. And she had saved my life.

"On the ship she gave coordinates for Galor. Then stood to one side, out of the way of those working. For this part of the trip I assigned young Pok to the communications console.

"After an hour I turned to my navigator, ChaqI. 'How long to Galor?'

"'If the human's coordinates were correct,' ChaqI said, 'within three hours.'

"From where she stood, the singer said, 'The human's coordinates are correct. I hope your navigation is as good.'

"I laughed. This human singer knew Klingons. She knew how to respond to a Klingon's challenge. I liked her. I turned to her. 'We should be overtaking his ship shortly. What kind of weapons does it have?'

" 'Nothing a Bird of Prey can't handle,' she said.

"Again, I trusted her. There was no need to ask more.

"A short time later, Pok said, 'Picking up a ship, within sensor range. At warp six point five.'

" 'Details.' I ordered.

"A moment later Pok listed the ship's configuration. The singer had been correct. If the ship in front of us belonged to the bartender, it was no match for my ship.

" 'That's him,' the singer said after she heard the ship's description.

" 'Engaging cloaking device,' ChaqI said.

" 'No!' I said. 'I want him to feel us breathing down his neck. Increase speed.'

"A few moments later young Pok at communications said, 'Sir. They are hailing us.'

" 'On screen,' I ordered.

"After a moment the image on the main screen changed to a picture of the face of the bartender. He smiled, then noticed that the singer had moved up to a position behind me.

" 'Hello, Gowron,' he said. 'I see you've picked up a new bed partner.'

" 'It is over, Meska,' I said. 'We have found you. Do not sacrifice your crew. Come aboard my ship. Meet your death honorably.'

"The bartender glanced at the singer behind me, then back at me. 'I have no intention of dying.'

"I glanced back at the singer. She shrugged. 'His weapons are useless from this distance.'

"I turned back to the bartender. I was puzzled at his attitude, but I did not let it show. 'You are outgunned. You cannot outrun us. I will destroy your vessel and everyone aboard.'

"The bartender laughed. 'I don't think so, Gowron.'

"'Your confidence does not fit your situation. You are either insane or simply a fool.'

"Again the bartender laughed. 'Do you think I am foolish enough to work alone? I have a man aboard your ship.'

"This time it was my turn to laugh. 'T'lak. He is dead. Lying in his own blood on the floor of your bar. Like so much litter.'

"'Really?' the bartender said. But the news did not seem to reduce his confidence.

"'Surrender, now,' I said.

"'T'lak was with you for some time,' the bartender said, staring intensely at me. 'Who knows what other betrayals he might be guilty of. Sabotage, perhaps?'

"Then the bartender nodded, his gaze focused on a place over my shoulder. I should have understood at that moment, but I did not.

"Suddenly a loud beeping started. A beeping not normally heard on my ship.

"'Over there,' the singer said, pointing at a panel. I rushed to the location of the beeping, but ChaqI beat me there. He pulled off the panel. In an area mostly hidden from view I saw that a detonator was making the loud sound. With the loud beeping, it obviously was made to be found when triggered. Therefore, it

STAR TREK

was intended for other uses besides blowing up the ship.

"The detonator was keyed to a pad with five numbers. Obviously a certain code had to be punched in to deactivate it.

"ChaqI inspected the detonator quickly, then glanced up at me. 'It is connected to the antimatter containment field.'

"'Shields are dropping,' Pok yelled.

"I turned. The singer had moved to ChaqI's panel and lowered the shields.

"'Stop her,' I ordered.

"Pok and D'cIq at once moved from their stations toward her, but she yelled out, 'Now!'

"A transporter beam took her.

"Before my men could stop her.

"They stopped as she vanished, and quickly returned to their posts.

"Then I heard the bartender laughing again on the main screen. I turned to see the singer now standing beside him. I had been completely taken into another of the bartender's traps. I could feel my anger. These two would die. I would see to that.

"'Pok. Take navigation. Close in on the ship. Engage tractor beam.'

"I faced the screen. 'Bartender. Singer. This changes nothing. I will still destroy your ship.'

"'Kill us,' the singer said, 'and you will be dead in minutes. That detonator is set on a timer.' She smiled at me. 'Now. You promise to let us go, and I will give you the correct sequence you need to disarm it.'

126

"I turned my back on her.

"Pok was following my orders. I moved to ChaqI's side over the detonator. 'How does it work?'

"He pointed to the pad of five keys. 'This is the arming function. Once it has been set, you must tap in the correct sequence of keys to disarm it.' Softly he said, 'There is no other way.'

"'Time is running out, Gowron,' the singer said on the screen behind me.

"I ignored her.

"'ChaqI. Is there any way to determine the sequence?'

"He shook his head just enough for me to see.

"Behind me the singer said, 'You do not understand, Gowron. I *have* the sequence.'

"I turned to Pok. 'Release the tractor beam.'

"'At last,' the singer said. 'I knew you would see it my way, Gowron.'

"'Lock disrupters on target,' I ordered.

"'Wha . . .' the singer seemed to gasp. 'Wait!'

"I raised my hand, ready to give the order to fire. If we were to die, at least I would take the knowledge that the person responsible had paid the price.

"And also that I killed the person who killed my friend.

"'He's bluffing,' the bartender said. He was still smiling. 'They won't do it.'

"'Idiot!' the singer shouted at him. 'You don't understand Klingons.'

"The bartender laughed at her. 'This is not one of your Klingon operas.'

"The singer held up her hand to me. 'Wait!'

"I paused a moment longer.

"She was clearly panicked. She knew she was about to die.

"'You want to know who hired us?' she asked. 'A Klingon. From Taganika. From an ancient house.'

"The bartender laughed. 'You embarrass yourself. He is bluffing.'

"The fool did not understand us. But I knew she did. At least enough to be worried.

"'You want a name, Gowron,' the singer said, ignoring the bartender and turning to face me. 'I can give you that. A name, in exchange for our lives.'

"I looked calmly at her. 'I have sworn a blood oath to kill you and all those responsible for the death of my friend Torghn. Your lives are not a negotiating point.'

"'But,' the singer said, 'if you kill us, you will die.'

"'Then let us all die together.'

"I dropped my hand. 'Fire.'

"Beside the singer the bartender suddenly realized he had made a mistake.

"A very large mistake.

"On the main screen the faces of the bartender and the singer were replaced by the beautiful scene of their ship exploding in a ball of white.

"We all saluted the explosion.

"All the crew said, *"pItlh."*

"Pok's voice was full and loud among the voices.

"I turned to the crew. 'The blood oath is obeyed.'

128

Klingon!

"ChaqI nodded. 'But the detonator.'

"I motioned for Pok. 'Come here.'

"I pointed to the pad inside the panel. 'Pok. We must disarm this detonator now. But only the correct sequence will work.'

"I filled my voice with confidence and turned to my bridge crew. 'None of us knows what that sequence is. Is that a correct assumption.'

"'Yes,' they all said at the same time.

"I motioned for young Pok to kneel down beside the panel. 'Punch in any sequence you feel is right. No one will blame you if you choose wrongly, Pok. We are prepared to die.'

"Pok looked nervous, as we all were. He studied the pad for a moment, then turned back to me. For a moment I thought fear had overcome him. But I was wrong.

"Very wrong.

"'Sir,' Pok said. 'The singer was responsible for this. Correct?'

"I nodded. 'It would seem such was true.'

"'The opera she sang,' Pok said. 'It has a theme. A simple theme.'

"'You waste time,' ChaqI said. 'Push the buttons. Enough talking. I am prepared to die.'

"I held up my hand for ChaqI to stop. I understood what Pok was thinking. It made as much sense as anything else.

"'Yes,' I said. "The opera has a theme."

"'A five-note theme,' Pok said. 'If I am correct.'

129

"I nodded. 'You are.'

" 'If you would, sir, assign each note a number from one to five,' Pok said. 'From low to high.'

"I hummed the simple theme of the opera, then said the numbers to Pok.

"He nodded and took a deep breath. Then he turned and without a moment's hesitation punched in the five numbers I had given him. His hand did not even shake. His father would have been so proud of him at that moment.

"The device gave out a series of musical beeps, following the theme of the opera, then went dead.

"The crew around the bridge yelled their joy. Many slapped Pok on the back, not even giving him time to stand. We were all prepared to die. But the quick thinking of a fellow warrior had saved us. That was a moment for rejoicing.

"And I joined in.

"Then I pulled Pok to his feet. I, too, slapped him on the back. 'The singer's aria from *qul tuq*. I should have thought of that myself.'

"I laughed. And Pok laughed with me. 'But I did not. I am glad you did, young Pok.'

"Pok only smiled. But I knew that in the last few moments he had grown to be a full warrior.

"I looked Pok in the face. 'We have killed the assassins who killed your father, Pok. Until we know who hired these assassins, the oath will not be fulfilled. We will find this Klingon from an ancient house.'

"Pok nodded.

"I shouted to my crew. 'Return to your stations. Set a course for Taganika.'"

Gowron glanced around at those at the table as he took a drink of his ale.

Picard had managed to finish most of his salad. And it looked as if most of the others also were almost done. But Gowron clearly had another part of the story he wanted to tell this lunch hour. And after his long drink he immediately started in again.

"The trip back to Taganika, even at full warp, gave us all enough time for dinner. I went with Pok to the mess. As we entered, Pok saw the old Klingon and approached him.

"I could see as the old warrior looked up that he had a weary look in his eyes. He clearly thought this was finished between himself and young Pok. He knew he had lost. What more was there to determine?

"But Pok surprised him. He simply placed a writing pad down on the table in front of the old warrior, then without a word moved to get food.

"We filled our plates and returned to the table as the old Klingon finished reading what Pok had given him. He placed the pad on the table as if it burned his hands. Then he sat staring at it, as if he didn't know what to do.

"ChaqI sat down across from the old warrior and leaned forward. 'What does it say?'

" 'The words are not for me to read aloud,' the old Klingon said. His voice was soft. Very soft.

"I sat down next to ChaqI and took the pad. I glanced at what Pok had done. 'Pok has written a *GaTH'k*,' I said, loud enough for all in the mess to hear my voice. 'An ode of respect for the old Klingon, Ler'at.'

"I turned to ChaqI. 'Ler'at is full of old superstitions,' I said. 'He believes it is bad luck to speak proud words about yourself. I will read them.'

"That got a cheer of agreement from those in the mess. The old Klingon said nothing. His gaze stayed focused on the table in front of him.

"So I read Pok's words.

'Ler'at, House of Tignar. Warrior Son.
At the battle of teh, he killed many men.
At the battle of reth he took many hurts.
His arms were strong to lift the Bat'tleh high.'

"I paused, then went on.

'His heart was fierce to keep the enemy afraid.
At teh, at reth, at lagon, at dumath, at negan.
His arms are heavy now with the weight of many
battles.
His heart is burdened by the press of many honors.
When he dies, the heaven will shake
with the screams of his comrades.
Warning the dead, Beware! Beware!
A warrior is coming.'

"I laid the pad down in front of the old Klingon and he picked it up. The room was silent with respect for what we had all just heard.

"The old Klingon stood and moved around the table. He placed a hand on Pok's shoulder. 'May you die with honor, Pok.'

"Then the old Klingon left the mess quickly.

"I turned to young Pok. 'This was a true *GaTH'k*, Pok.'

"The others in the room agreed, some loudly. Then all went back to their eating.

"In a quieter voice I said to Pok, 'I see the makings of a warrior poet in you. It runs in your family's blood. Your father was also very good at—'

"Before I could go any further, the communications officer announced we were approaching Taganika.

"I broke off my sentence and stood. 'Come,' I said to young Pok. 'We are almost there. Prepare yourself for your return to your home as a warrior.' "

Gowron looked around at this audience again. "It seems we must return to our meeting. The time grows short."

Admiral Jellico stood. "Yes, it would seem that way."

"I look forward to hearing the conclusion of your story," Picard said as he stood with Gowron. And he did. He had no idea just how the story was going to end up. Or what part it played in the talks and events going on with the murders. But he suspected it did in a very large way.

"Tonight, Captain," Gowron said. "Tonight the story will find an end."

Picard nodded. "Good. I will be back here, waiting and listening."

"Yes," Gowron said. "I look forward to the nights. I have grown fond of this table. And the good company."

"I am honored," Picard said.

"As am I," Riker said.

Gowron laughed. "Tonight you will match me, glass for glass, Commander Riker."

Picard watched as Riker turned slightly pale at the thought of that much blood wine. Then he smiled. "I will match you, sir."

Gowron laughed. "True Klingon spirit. I like that in a human."

Chapter Fourteen

"YOUR CHOICE THIS TIME," Lieutenant Jadzia Dax said, smiling. Behind her the others filed out of the afternoon meeting, talking among themselves. She had come over to Riker after the meeting and asked him if he'd like a third try at dinner.

He'd gladly accepted.

Now he smiled at her, then decided. "Quark's again. Last time I didn't have to pay for the dinner I had there."

"If I remember," she said, "didn't you pay with a headache?"

He waved her comment aside. "I have paid for many a visit to a bar with a headache."

She laughed and took his arm, turning him toward the door. "Then Quark's it is."

But this time they didn't even get seated before

their dinner was interrupted. As they were entering Quark's Riker felt the familiar sensation of being transported.

"What?" Dax said, turning toward him, a look of alarm on her face. Obviously, people being beamed out of the middle of the station was not a normal occurence.

"Sorry," he managed to say to her.

Now the question was, just where was he going? And who was taking him?

Major Kira stood at the security console as the lift brought Chancellor Gowron, Captain Picard, Lieutenant Worf, Admiral Jellico, Commander Sisko, and three guards to Ops.

As they continued toward the transporter pad, she checked security measures. Everything seemed to be in order. She also did a quick check to make sure the two Cardassian ships were still in their positions. In almost two days they hadn't moved. And Gul Dukat had not even called the station. It was very odd. Very odd indeed.

Gowron laughed. "Admiral Jellico," he said. "I would be very proud to show you my ship."

Kira couldn't hear Jellico's answer, but the admiral stepped up on the platform next to Gowron and his two guards.

"Captain," Gowron said loudly to Captain Picard. "Are you sure you would not like to join us?"

Captain Picard shook his head no. Kira heard him

say, "Thank you, Gowron. "But I have duties to attend to on the *Enterprise.*"

Gowron smiled. "A captain's work, huh, Picard. Worf?"

"No, sir. Thank you," Worf said.

Kira did not hear Picard's response, but Gowron laughed. Maybe this laughter meant the afternoon's meetings had gone better. Kira hoped so. It would be a shame to have all this effort go to waste.

"Ready," Gowron said.

Commander Sisko turned to her. "Lower shields."

She did as she was ordered. Gowron opened his communicator. "Four to transport. *DaH!*"

Suddenly the board in front of Kira went crazy. Two new Klingon Birds of Prey decloaked right in front of the station.

One fired on Gowron's flagship. The other stood off to one side.

"Shields up!" Sisko shouted. "Red alert!"

Kira's actions were automatic as she triggered the red alert and brought the shields up. The weapons were instantly set to ready and brought up to power.

But it was too late to stop the transport. The four on the transporter pad disappeared, only Kira did not like what her instruments had shown.

"Sir," Kira said, doing her best to make her voice remain calm. "They did not transport to Gowron's ship."

"What?" both Picard and Sisko said at the same time.

"When the Bird of Prey fired on Gowron's ship, its shields went up automatically. The transport was not done by that ship."

"So where did they go?" Sisko demanded, stepping toward her.

Kira let her fingers dance over her board. It took only a moment to have the answer. "Sir. They were taken to the second new Klingon ship."

On the large screen Kira watched in shock as the two new Klingon ships quickly turned to move away without firing another shot. They again cloaked, disappearing almost as fast as they had appeared.

Again things around Kira seemed to happen at once.

Gul Dukat's ship turned and shot off in the direction it seemed the two Klingon ships had gone. The other Cardassian ship stayed in position.

Picard tapped his com badge. *"Enterprise.* Lock on Commander Riker, Lieutenant Worf, and myself and beam us directly to the bridge. Now!"

"Shields down," Sisko ordered.

Kira instantly dropped the shields, and a moment later Picard and Worf disappeared.

"Shields back up," Sisko ordered, and Kira did as she was told.

Then the two of them stood and watched as first Gowron's flagship, and then, a moment later, the *Enterprise* turned and jumped to warp.

Both of them stood there for a moment in silence. Then Sisko said, "Stand down from red alert. Take us to yellow."

"Yes, sir," Kira said.

"Now," Sisko said. "We have a Klingon somewhere on this station who doesn't belong here. I want him found. I want you, Dax, and Odo in my office in five minutes."

"Yes, sir," Kira said. But at that moment she had no idea how she was going to follow that order. Since this morning before the meetings, over forty Klingons had beamed aboard the station. Which one didn't belong?

She was about to call for Dax when she burst off the turbo lift. "What happened? Riker was beamed off the Promenade."

"I know," Kira said. She looked up at the screen showing only one Klingon Bird of Prey and one Cardassian ship left in positions around the station.

Dax followed her gaze, then said, "Oh, my."

Chapter Fifteen

RIKER WENT FROM LOOKING at Jadzia Dax's beautiful but shocked face to staring at the bridge of the *Enterprise*.

Beside him Captain Picard and Worf materialized at the same time.

"Red alert," Picard instantly said, moving to a position in front of the screen. Worf scrambled instantly to his station at security.

It seemed they both knew exactly what was going on. Riker wanted very much to ask what happened, but he knew he would get filled in after just a moment. He moved over to his position beside the captain.

The red alert lights came up.

On screen Gowron's flagship turned and quickly dropped into warp, disappearing off in a direction headed for the Klingon Empire.

"Stay with that ship, Mister Data. Engage."

"Yes, sir," Data said. A moment later Riker watched as they turned and went to warp nine.

"Where is Gul Dukat's ship?" Picard asked.

Data glanced at his board. "On this same heading, sir. A few minutes ahead of Gowron's ship."

"Any sign of the other two ships?"

"No sir," Data said. "They remain cloaked."

Picard nodded and turned and sat down. "Well, then. We'll just have to trust that either the Cardassians or Gowron's crew have a way of tracking a ship under cloak."

Riker moved to Picard's side and sat down. After a moment of sitting there beside Picard with nothing seeming to be happening at once, he asked, "What happened?"

Picard glanced at him, then smiled a half smile, understanding that Riker had no idea what had gone on. "Gowron and Admiral Jellico have been kidnapped."

Picard must have assumed that was enough information, since he turned back to the main screen and stared at the stars streaking past.

Riker felt his stomach clamp into a tight knot as the captain's words slowly sank in.

And he felt downright queasy as the implications of

what had happened sank in. The sector was now, very suddenly, poised on the brink of war.

And it was up to them to stop it.

dRacLa, son of Vok, walked along the Promenade toward Quark's bar. A dozen other Klingon warriors walked on the Promenade. For at least the moment, he didn't stand out. He needed both food and drink. He also needed news. He wasn't sure that his message had gotten out of the station. And if Lursa had received it. If it had, he would move to step two of his plan.

It appeared that the afternoon's meetings had just broken up. Many Klingons were around and none seemed to be in the slightest bit alarmed. It was clear nothing had happened. Yet. But if it was to happen, it would be anytime now.

He quickly moved into Quark's and to the bar. A small Ferengi came to a place in front of him.

"What can I get for you, fine sir?" the Ferengi asked, an annoying smile on its face.

"Ale, first. Then a full loaf of Klingon bread."

"Strange diet," the Ferengi said, and moved off.

dRacLa turned and stood watching out over the bar. There was no one in the room he recognized. And that was good. No one would know him.

Two Federation officers were entering. Suddenly one of them was beamed out, almost in midstride. The other looked very shocked, then turned and headed off down the Promenade at a run.

It seemed now, that something had happened. Something very important.

He laughed to himself as the Ferengi slid the ale in front of him.

"You like your own jokes," the Ferengi said. "You ought to hear mine."

"Can you hurry the bread, Ferengi?" He laid an Acta crystal on the bar.

The Ferengi's eyes opened slightly, then he said, "Sure. Sure," and moved quickly down the bar.

Around the bar a few of the warriors suddenly answered their communications calls. The word passed quickly. Within moments every Klingon in the room got up and headed for the door.

"Wow," the Ferengi said, staring at all the warriors running for the door. He dropped the bread on the table. "What's the rush?"

"Called back to our ships," dRacLa said. He slid the crystal at the Ferengi, then downed his ale. With the bread tucked under his arm he followed the rest of his Klingon brothers out of the bar.

But near a side corridor he turned left and slipped unseen into the many halls of the huge station.

Gowron glanced around at the darkened room he found himself in after transport. He had expected to find himself on his transport platform in his own ship.

But instead, he and his guards and Admiral Jellico were transported into a small, dark room, with the doors closed and very securely latched. He knew the room was on a Bird of Prey. But he also knew he wasn't on his own ship.

"What?" Jellico said. "Is this . . ."

"Where is this place?" Gowron called out.

When no answer came back, he indicated to the door. "Get us out of here. *moD!*"

RocIa and uQvam, his guards, both instantly pulled their disrupters.

RocIa adjusted the setting on his. Then he pointed it at the locking mechanism on the door. His shot made no impact. It became instantly clear that the walls were protected by a forcefield. There would be no breaking out.

"bup," he ordered his guard. "We will wait."

Both guards kept their weapons drawn, as they should have done, and took up positions flanking him.

Admiral Jellico finally managed to find his voice. "What happened?"

"It seems, Admiral," Gowron said, "that we have been taken hostage."

"But who would want to take me?" he asked, glancing around. "For what reason?"

Gowron forced himself to not laugh. "Admiral. I am afraid you are just an unlucky passenger. This is a Klingon ship. I fear this is a plan to kill me." He glanced around the small room. "And it may well succeed."

"How can such a thing happen?" Jellico asked. "And why. Who would do this?"

This time Gowron could not hold back his laughter.

"Admiral, have you not been listening to my story of Pok?"

The admiral looked at the Klingon chancellor for a moment, then nodded. "Yes. But I thought that was only a story."

"Admiral," Gowron said. "The story was truth. I said as much. There is always meaning beyond a Klingon's story."

He turned away from the stupid human and moved to the wall. "Now," he said to the admiral. "I suggest you get comfortable. We may have a long wait."

With that, Gowron put his back against the wall and slid to the floor. In front of him his two guards took up their positions. They would give their life for him. He hoped it would not come to that.

Chapter Sixteen

LURSA GLANCED AT HER SISTER, who stood beside her, intently watching the screen. Then she, too, went back to watching. They were at warp eight, maximum velocity under cloak. They were heading into Klingon territory. Gowron and his guards had been beamed directly into a room on the *Botka,* which traveled close beside them.

They were both traveling under cloak. Yet behind them followed three ships. The Cardassian Gul Dukat's ship, Gowron's flagship, and the Federation ship *Enterprise.* And all three were overtaking them quickly.

"How can they know we are here?" B'Etor asked for the fifth time.

For the first four times neither Lursa nor any of the crew had an answer. Yet it seemed their pursuers did know exactly where they were. She had already made two course corrections. But each time Dukat's ship followed exactly. And Gowron's flagship and the *Enterprise* did the same. This made no sense.

And it could not be happening. Their ship was cloaked. Not even another Klingon ship could accurately follow a cloaked Bird of Prey.

"Alter course again," Lursa ordered. "Two degrees, then bring us back on heading."

The other ships followed as if she were making the turns in plain sight.

"They will catch us shortly," B'Etor said. "What then? We can't stay ahead of them if we are cloaked."

"We fight," Lursa said. "And when we die, Gowron dies with us."

"So be it," B'Etor said.

"So be it," Lursa repeated. "But I have another idea first."

"Captain," Worf said. "It is possible the Cardassians are working with the enemies of the Empire."

Riker glanced around to where Worf stood, intently watching the path of the two ships in front of them. Riker had thought of the same thing, as he was sure Picard had also. This might just be Gul Dukat's way of leading Gowron's ship and the *Enterprise* into a wild ride across space.

But on the other hand, if Dukat truly did have a way of tracking a cloaked ship accurately, at these speeds he might be Gowron and Admiral Jellico's only hope.

"I know, Mister Worf," Captain Picard said. "Continue following, Mister Data."

"Yes, sir," Data said. "Dukat is changing course again."

"Stay with him."

"Ten minutes and we'll be into the neutral zone," Worf said.

Suddenly ahead of them the scene changed. What had simply been three ships following in close order became five as two Klingon Birds of Prey decloaked. They were a surprisingly close distance ahead of Dukat's ship.

"That answers the question of Dukat being able to follow a cloaked ship," Riker said. "But I wonder how he managed that trick?"

"I'd like to know that myself," Picard said. "And about a thousand other people in Starfleet."

"The two Birds of Prey are accelerating," Data said. "They are now at warp nine point one."

"Go to warp nine point two. Stay with them, Mister Data," Picard said.

"They are sending a subspace message ahead of them. They are calling for help."

Riker glanced over at Picard, but he showed no emotion. If extra Birds of Prey came into the fight, this might get out of hand very quickly. And there was no way of knowing just how many ships would come to such a call.

"Any other starships near here?" Picard asked.

"No, sir," Worf said. "The closest is the *Merrimac,* a good five hours away."

Picard nodded and said nothing.

"Gowron's ship is also calling ahead for help," Worf said.

"We're going to have a Klingon civil war," Riker said. He just couldn't believe this was happening. He should be having a relaxed, fun dinner with Jadzia Dax at this very moment.

"Let's see if we can stop that war from developing," Picard said. "And any other war, for that matter. Mister La Forge?"

"Go ahead, sir." Geordi La Forge's voice came back strong over the comm.

"How much harder can we push this?"

"For a short time I can give you warp nine-four, sir," Geordi said. "But I can't promise you too much more than that."

"Do it," Picard said. "Mister Data, warp nine point four. I want to be on top of those two Birds of Prey."

"Yes, sir," Data said.

On screen the ships in front of them visibly moved closer. Within a few seconds the *Enterprise* moved past both Gowron's flagship and Dukat's ship as if it was passing them in a race.

"Mister Worf. I want you to target both ships at the same time. Slow them down, without destroying them. We don't know where Chancellor Gowron and Admiral Jellico are."

"Understood, sir," Worf said.

A moment later Worf said, "In range, sir."

"Fire." Picard said.

Chancellor Gowron had spent the time in the darkened room ignoring Admiral Jellico and listening to the ship around him. He knew they were traveling under cloak. And at top speed under cloak.

Then, when the sound changed faintly, he knew the cloak had been dropped. And he could hear the engines being pushed even harder. His guess would have been over warp nine.

It took him a moment to understand why. Why a cloaked ship would need extra speed, more than being cloaked. Then he understood. Someone had been tracking the cloaked ship since they left the station.

He suddenly laughed aloud, understanding exactly what had happened. And most likely, how.

"What's so funny?" Admiral Jellico asked. Gowron could not miss the sneer in the admiral's voice.

"Our enemies are stupid," Gowron said. "Their stupidity may yet get us killed. But they are stupid, so our chances of living are better."

"How do you know that, sitting in here?" Jellico asked, staring at Gowron.

"I have ears, Admiral," Gowron said. Then, turning directly to look at the admiral, the head of the Klingon High Council said, "And I know how to listen."

Before Admiral Jellico could respond, the ship was rocked. Gowron rolled with the first impact and came to his feet, braced against a wall for the next.

"Watch the door. If the field drops, I want out of here. Quickly."

Both guards nodded their understanding.

Again the ship rocked with another hit. Admiral Jellico tried to hang on, but he fought the movement and ended up banging his arm and head against the wall. He was not knocked out. But he could not walk.

Gowron ignored him. There would be time for him if they lived through this. Instead Gowron kept listening.

"We have slowed," he said after another moment.

Another blast rocked the ship and the lights flickered. Instantly both his guards fired at the door and it swung open.

"Good," Gowron said. He took the disrupter from RocIa and indicated that the guard should pick up the stunned admiral and bring him along. Then without so much as a glance backward he was out the door.

"Fire again, Mister Worf," Captain Picard ordered.

Again the blue beams of the phasers shot out at both Klingon Birds of Prey.

"Direct hits," Worf said. "They are losing power and slowing."

Two phaser bursts shot from one of the Birds of Prey, and the *Enterprise* rocked.

"Shields holding," Data said.

"Warn the other two ships to stand clear and not fire," Picard said.

"One ship is again trying to power up," Worf said.

"Hit them again," Picard said.

Again two blasts of phaser fire shot out, wrapping the Klingon ship into a ball of fire.

"They have lost power," Worf said.

"The two ships are slowly moving apart," Data said. "In less than thirty seconds the second ship will be out of our range."

"Stay with this one," Picard said. "Inform Gowron's ship of our decision."

A moment later Data said, "Done, sir. Gowron's ship is moving after the other. Dukat is remaining outside the fight."

Picard nodded. "Smart man, Dukat. He's just letting the enemies fight."

"He brought us here to fight his battle," Riker said.

"That he did," Picard said. "That he did."

Chapter Seventeen

GOWRON LED THE WAY into the hall. A disrupter blast almost caught him, missing his right ear by a very small distance. He rolled to the left against the corridor wall and came up firing. His shot took down the one guard without problem.

"He should have learned to fire more accurately," Gowron said, standing over the body.

uQvam laughed, but kept the hall behind Gowron under surveillance.

"We go to the bridge," Gowron said. He took the guard's gun and gave it to RocIa, who shifted the admiral on his shoulder slightly and tucked the gun in his belt.

Gowron turned and headed off toward the lift. Over his shoulder he said to RocIa, "Along the way I know where we can stash some baggage."

"That would be helpful," RocIa said, shifting the weight of the admiral again slightly on his shoulder.

Admiral Jellico only grunted.

They left the admiral in a large storage closet with the warning that he should remain very quiet. He nodded his understanding before Gowron shut the closet door on him.

Then, as they moved the final distance to the turbo lift, Gowron said softly to his guards. "I have had a desire to do that to him. All week."

This time both guards laughed.

A few moments later they crouched on the lift as it neared the bridge level. Gowron could see a faint haze of smoke and the alert lights blinking. He knew the crew were frantically working to get their ship working. And were guarding against an attack from the outside. He doubted they had been alerted to their escape. They would never expect an attack from within.

With a nod, Gowron and his two guards stood. "Surrender!" he called out in a loud, solid voice. They stepped off the lift onto the bridge. "Or die."

Three of the Klingons at their stations went for weapons, but Gowron and his men already had their disrupters drawn. The others never fired even one shot.

The navigator and the captain both raised their hands in surrender.

Gowron walked up to the captain. He knew the man. cha'DIch, son of hiJaK. Gowron personally had given him his command on this very ship.

"You dishonor yourself, cha'DIch," Gowron said. "Working for the House of Duras. And against the Empire."

The man said nothing.

"Your weapon," Gowron said, holding out his hand.

The captain's hand went slowly to his side, then quickly drew out his disrupter.

Gowron cut him down before the disrupter even got above his belt.

The man fell to the floor, and Gowron used his foot to turn him over to make sure he was dead. Then to the man's face he said, "Stupidity does not make up for a lack of honor."

He turned to his guards. "Can you bring up the screens?"

One guard moved quickly to a console and a moment later the front screen showed the *Starship Enterprise* at close range.

"Picard," Gowron said to himself. "You should have been born a Klingon. You would have given us much honor."

Lursa stared at the scene in front of her. The *Botka* seemed to be heavily damaged. The Federation ship *Enterprise* hung near it. They had also taken some damage, but not as bad as the *Botka*. Smoke filled the bridge and made her choke slightly. But she refrained from coughing.

Gowron's ship stayed close to hers as they slowly drifted away from the *Botka* and the *Enterprise*.

"We will have warp power again momentarily," B'Etor said. "And the cloaking device still works."

"Good news," Lursa said. "But play dead for the moment. Just keep the shields up."

"Understood," her navigator said.

B'Etor moved up to her side. "Sister. What are you thinking?"

"I am thinking," Lursa said, "that the Cardassian ship had planted a device on the *Botka* that allowed them to track us. Possibly with Gowron's party."

"Since Gowron is there, and we are here . . ." B'Etor said.

She did not need to say any more. Lursa turned to her engineer. "Can you give me warp three? Under cloak."

He glanced at his instruments, then nodded. "Yes. But we will need repairs shortly."

Lursa nodded. "On my command," she said.

The *Botka* is hailing the *Enterprise,*" B'Etor said.

"Now!" Lursa said. *"nom!"*

"Sir," Data said. "We are being hailed."

Before Picard could answer, Worf said, "Sir. The other ship has again jumped to warp and cloaked."

Picard glanced up at the screen. Gowron's ship was not following it. And neither was Gul Dukat's. It seemed that whatever Dukat could track had been on the ship that was hailing them. He just hoped Gowron and the admiral were on this ship.

"Nothing we can do now about that one," Picard said. "On screen."

Gowron's smiling face lit up the screen. Behind him Picard could see his two guards at the consoles. And two bodies were in sight on the floor. Picard had no doubt that other bodies were close by.

"Thank you, Captain," Gowron said. "For your help."

Picard nodded. "It is good to see you well, my friend. And the admiral?"

Gowron smiled. "He bumped his head and is resting below."

Picard decided at that moment it was better to not ask. He had a hunch he would find out the entire story later.

"Your ship is approaching," Picard said.

Gowron glanced at his screen and then nodded. "I will return to the station shortly. It seems we have more than one story to finish this evening."

Picard laughed. "It would seem that way. Picard out."

Chapter Eighteen

THE VOYAGE BACK to *Deep Space Nine* took considerably longer than the flight away. Picard sat in his command chair most of the three hours, simply staring at the stars through the main screen. He didn't feel like resting just yet, even though the evening was growing late. Commander Riker sat beside him, also seemingly lost in his own thoughts. The rest of the bridge crew did their jobs quietly, giving him the time. He was grateful.

Shadowing the *Enterprise* were both Gul Dukat's ship and Gowron's flagship. Picard had talked to neither ship, although he knew he needed at least to acknowledge Dukat's help. He had not yet decided on the right words.

Admiral Jellico had been brought aboard the *Enterprise* and Dr. Crusher had checked him over, fixed his mild concussion, and sent him to sleep for the evening.

The captured Klingon ship had been taken under control by two of Gowron's fleet ships. The call for help from the House of Duras ships, it seemed, was never answered. Or at least was canceled by the ship that had escaped. How Gowron would handle the entire situation when he got back to Qu'onos was beyond imagining. Picard would probably never know.

He did know they had escaped both a sectorwide war, and a Klingon civil war. But it had been much too close a call.

For most of the last three hours his focus had been on trying to rescue something from the summit meetings. Somewhere there was a common ground between the Federation and the Klingon Empire. Today had shown that.

He stood and paced in front of the main screen.

He knew the answer was right in front of him. He just couldn't see it. The frustration was eating at him like a bad hunger. And there was only the meetings tomorrow and then it would be too late for this attempt.

The last few hours had seen a Cardassian ship, a Klingon ship, and a Federation ship work together to solve a problem. There was something deep inside him that liked that fact. It felt right, as if these three races almost belonged working together. Yet he knew that was a very distant, and idealistic, dream.

After a moment of pacing Riker said, "Looking for a solution to the meetings deadlock, sir?"

Picard stopped and stared at the smiling Commander Riker. It was as if he'd been reading his mind.

"I've been doing the same thing, sir."

"Any solutions?"

Riker's response gladdened Picard's heart. "Yes, sir, I think I might have an idea."

Picard moved over and sat back down, turned to face Riker in his command chair.

"Sir," Riker said. "I think the answer lies in the story Gowron has been telling. Even Admiral Jellico has been interested."

"Go on," Picard said. His instinct told him Riker was on the right track.

"I think we should convince Gowron to finish his story at lunch tomorrow," Riker said. "And in the meantime I'll talk to Geordi about the possibility of turning Gowron's story into a holodeck program to train Federation personnel. See where the problems might lie."

Picard nodded. "Interesting." He let the Riker's words sink in for a moment, then went on. "I knew that Gowron was telling his story for another reason. But even I have learned things about the Klingons from it. It just might work as a training program."

"Exactly," Riker said. "It might not be the diplomatic breakthrough we had all hoped for. But it will be a link to train Federation personnel. And something we can take out of these meetings to point to as progress."

"And possibly the Klingons could have a story of ours," Picard said, smiling. "To help them understand us."

Riker laughed. "That, sir, would have to be one very interesting story."

"We have them, Number One," Picard said. "We have them."

"Sir," Data said. "We are within range of *Deep Space Nine.*"

"Hail them, Mister Data," Picard said.

He again stood, pulled his shirt into place, and faced the screen as Commander Sisko's smiling face came on-screen.

"Permission to resume our position?" Picard asked.

"Granted," Sisko said. "And welcome back."

"It's good to be back," Picard said. And he meant it. "I will see you before tomorrow's meeting."

"I look forward to it," Sisko said.

"Picard out."

"Mister Data," Picard said, not turning from the main screen that now showed the station. Dukat's ship had moved back into a place near the other Cardassian ship. "Hail Gul Dukat."

"Aye, sir," Data said.

A moment later the main screen was filled with Gul Dukat's smiling face. He was sitting in his command chair, looking very relaxed and very happy with himself, as only a Cardassian can manage to look.

"Captain Picard," Dukat said, smiling even bigger.

"Gul Dukat," Picard said, nodding at the Cardassian. "I would like to officially express both my thanks and that of the Federation, for your help in this incident."

Dukat bowed forward slightly, acknowledging what Picard said and still smiling. "Captain," he said. "It was my pleasure. I can assure you of that."

"I have no doubt," Picard said.

Dukat laughed. "Maybe next time my warnings will be taken seriously."

"Dukat," Picard said, ignoring the last remark. "I would be very much interested in discovering how you were able to follow the cloaked ship."

The Cardassian Gul laughed. "Secrets, Picard. A secret that must remain with me for the moment."

Picard smiled at him. "As you wish. Thank you again. Picard out."

Before the screen cut off, Dukat again nodded his acknowledgment. And then laughed.

Chapter Nineteen

Riker had only a moment to apologize to Dax for his hasty exit, before the morning's session started. During the meeting Admiral Jellico seemed to be even more subdued and angry. Nothing was accomplished, as Riker had figured would happen.

But as to Gowron's story being made into a holodeck program, Geordi had said there would be few problems and Riker had relayed the news to Captain Picard. He had only nodded, as if he had expected as much.

Earlier Captain Picard had met with Commander Sisko about the murder and bombing. He said nothing about that discussion, either.

Right before the lunch break Captain Picard had asked Gowron if he would mind finishing his story over their food. Gowron had readily agreed.

Riker made sure he was walking from the meeting to Quark's bar with Dax. "Did you end up having any dinner?" she asked him as they followed Gowron and Picard from the room.

"Not really," he said. "Only a snack before bed."

She laughed. "Me too."

They walked in silence for a moment. Riker had hoped she would say something about dinner this evening. Captain Picard planned on having the *Enterprise* stay at *Deep Space Nine* until tomorrow. They had one more night. But so far she had said nothing. And after three attempts, he was almost afraid to ask. They had been having such bad luck.

Finally, as they neared Quark's, he cleared his throat. "Would you—"

"Yes," she said, quickly. Then she laughed. "Fourth time might be the charm."

"It just might be," he said.

And they both laughed.

It took only a few minutes for everyone to get settled again around the large table in the back of Quark's. Two Klingon guards stood facing the rest of the bar, hands behind their backs. Lieutenant Barclay and Worf joined them, with a special welcome from Gowron. Riker had a sneaking suspicion that Gowron actually liked Reg Barclay.

Quark and Rom took only a few more minutes to get the drinks and food on the table. After a moment it almost felt as if yesterday's events had not happened.

Gowron looked around. "You have been a good audience. A storyteller can ask for nothing more."

"Your story has kept us riveted," Captain Picard said. "As any good story does to an audience."

"Hear! Hear!" Riker said. And the rest of the table agreed. Even Admiral Jellico.

"Then," Gowron said, "the end of the story is at hand. I shall get to it."

"Night had just gripped Pok's home when we beamed down. His mother K'Tar greeted her warrior son as any mother would greet a son back from war. She hugged him. Her face shone.

"Then she nodded a thank-you to me. But no thanks were needed. I was grateful that Pok had come with me. For without his quick thinking, I would have been dead at the hands of my enemy.

"Qua'lon entered the greeting. Over drinks and food around their large dining room table I told our story up to that point. After I was finished I could see the joy shining from K'Tar's face.

"She touched the top of her son's hand. 'Your father would be proud of what you have done, Pok.'

" 'Agreed,' Qua'lon said. 'The circle of vengeance is closed. The House of SepIch can move on.'

" 'The circle is not closed,' I said. 'We must still find the murderer of Torghn.'

"Qua'lon stared at me, clearly not understanding. Or so I read his expression to mean.

" 'Qua'lon killed Vok,' K'Tar said, worry filling her

165

eyes. 'You have killed the assassins. Your traitorous guard is also dead. Who else do you expect to find?'

"'We still do not know who is behind this plot,' I said. 'The assassin said a Klingon—'

"'From an ancient house,' K'Tar said, finishing my sentence. 'It has to be Vok. He is of the House of Ingka. Other than the House of SepIch, no house on Taganika is as old. Who else would it be?'

"'So it would seem,' I said. 'I cannot explain. The circle does not feel complete to me.'

"'Gowron,' Qua'lon said, doing his best to comfort me. 'If you had been able to slay him with your own hands, as I did, you might feel different.'

"'Yes,' K'Tar said. 'It is finished.'

"'It is not finished, K'Tar!' a woman's voice said from near the front door. My guards were blocking her entrance. I recognized her as T'Var, wife of Vok.

"She stopped her struggles with my guards and looked at me. 'I would speak with Gowron.'

"Qua'lon jumped to his feet, clearly outraged. 'The wife of the *veQ* who killed my brother may not enter the House of SepIch.'

"She glared at Qua'lon, then spit on the floor. 'You *petaQ!* Your men have ransacked my home. Taken my belongings, my treasures, beaten my son, dRacLa.'

"'Fitting payment,' K'Tar said, 'for what your house has done to mine.'

"'My husband was innocent,' T'Var said. She again looked directly at me. 'Let me speak.'

"'As the head of the House of SepIch,' Qua'lon said, 'I refuse to allow you to speak.'

"'Qua'lon,' I said, my voice harsh.

"He turned to face me.

"'You are not the head of the House of SepIch. Pok is.'

"I turned to Pok, who had sat quietly through all this discussion, a trait of his that I admired. 'Pok?'

"'Let her speak,' Pok said.

"I motioned for my guard to let her enter and she came inside. I could tell from her look that she was not doing well. But I gave her none of my heart.

"Qua'lon sat down hard in his chair and roughly pushed his food plate away from himself, spilling his drink in his show of dislike for Pok's decision.

"'Speak, T'Var. You say Vok was innocent. Where is the proof you bring?'

"'Vok had no reason to kill Torghn,' T'Var said.

"'The probe was meant for me,' I said. 'Vok had many reasons to want me dead.'

"'True, Gowron,' T'Var said. 'My husband wanted you dead. I will not lie about that.'

"I nodded to her. 'Go on.'

"'My husband was no fool,' she said. 'Everyone knows what an honorable man Torghn was. He would never allow a guest, the head of the High Council of all guests, to be killed in his house. Think of the dishonor. He would die first. As he did.'

"'If a man wanted my husband dead,' K'Tar said, almost as if she were thinking out loud, 'he could aim at you, Gowron, and know my husband would take the death himself.'

"'And we would look for the man who would

murder me.' As if a light had been turned on in a dark room, the problem made sense to me.

"I turned to Pok. 'Who knew your father well enough to know this, Pok? And who would gain the most from Torghn's death?'

"He and I both glanced around the room. 'The House of SepIch is an ancient house, too. Is there a murderer among us. Pok?'"

Gowron stared at Barclay, who once again seemed to be caught by surprise at Gowron's attention. He glanced at Riker, then at the captain. Both showed no sign of expression, so he turned back to Gowron.

"I–I–I don't unders–s–stand?"

"Have you been listening?" Gowron asked. "Or just eating?"

"L–L–Listening, sir," Barclay said, glancing down at his mostly full plate of salad.

"Well then," Gowron said, pushing his empty dish away and leaning forward. "Who would Pok accuse? Anyone? Who wanted Torghn of the House of SepIch dead?"

"Y–y–you certainly did not," Barclay said.

Gowron laughed. "You speak the truth. I would have nothing to gain from Torghn's death. He was my ally in that area of the Empire." Gowron pulled out his knife and twisted it in his hands.

Then he stuck it into the table in front of Barclay, causing the lieutenant suddenly to scoot back away from the table.

"And if I did want him dead, I would have killed him in open view. That is my way."

Barclay nodded, never taking his gaze off the knife stuck in front of him.

After a moment Riker felt bad for Barclay's tension. He leaned to the side and whispered to him, "Who else in that room might have done it?"

Gowron smiled at Barclay as he looked up into his eyes. "H–H–His wife would also have n–n–no reason to kill her husband."

Gowron nodded. "Again correct. And if Pok had accused his own mother she would have drawn her knife, like I just did, and given it to her son. She would have told him to fulfill his blood oath. Then she would have offered her chest. But I never would have let him kill her.

"W–why?" Barclay asked.

"Honor," Gowron said. "Dishonor would have fallen on Pok's house for ten generations. The House of SepIch would have disappeared from memory. That would not be the way."

Barclay nodded. "V–V–Vok's wife T'Var was also in the room."

Gowron nodded. "She was. But she would have no more reason to kill Torghn than her husband. And she never would have done so."

"Then," Barclay said. "Qua'lon, Torghn's brother, is all that is left. Did he do it?"

Gowron held up his hand. "You jump ahead of the story, my friend." But that is the same conclusion that Pok came to that evening.

Gowron finished his ale, then held up his glass. "Blood wine, Ferengi!" He shouted across the bar. "I am about to finish a story. This water-filled ale will not do."

Riker glanced down at his plate. He had been so focused on listening to Gowron's story, he had forgotten to finish his salad. He took another bite and then pushed it aside. He wanted his attention on Gowron's story.

Even Admiral Jellico seemed to be taking the break in the story as a chance to finish lunch. If Captain Picard took his suggestion and proposed this story as a Holodeck training program, it would be wonderful. And very useful. Riker decided right at that moment that he would even offer to help on the production of such a program if it happened.

Quark served the glass of blood wine to Gowron. He took a long drink, then sighed. "Storytelling is best done with blood wine. It is my rule. And a good one."

Around the table all laughed.

Gowron turned to Barclay. "I told you Pok looked at Qua'lon, then pointed to him in response to my question."

Barclay nodded.

"Good," Gowron said. "Now I will tell you what happened next."

" 'You accuse me!' Qua'lon shouted at Pok, standing and tipping his chair over in his anger. 'Of killing my own brother! Why? I gain nothing.'

"I answered for Pok. 'Nothing.' I said. 'Unless Pok were also dead. Then you would become the head of the House of SepIch.'

"'I deny it!' Qua'lon shouted. I could tell that at that moment he wanted to come over the table and kill me. And his nephew. His honor had been questioned.

"'A charge has been made,' I said. 'You must offer proof of your innocence.'

"Qua'lon glanced at those of us staring at him. Then he said, 'I will offer proof. I challenge my accuser to a *vItHay'*. A test of innocence.'

"'Or guilt,' I added.

"'Oh, no,' K'Tar said.

"I turned to Pok. 'You have made this accusation of your uncle. You must accept his challenge.'

"Pok nodded.

"I slapped him on the shoulder.

"Qua'lon stood and started to leave. 'My men will see that the chamber is prepared.'

"I stood quickly and blocked his way. 'No!' I said in his face. 'My men will see to it.'

"I turned to my guards. 'Do so.'

"Qua'lon stared at me but made no move to challenge me. At that moment he was thinking. For I would have gladly killed him where he stood.

"Barclay," Gowron said. "Do you know what a *vItHay'* is? And how it is performed?"

Barclay shook his head no.

Gowron turned to Riker. "Do you?"

"I do not, sir," Riker said.

Gowron glanced at first Worf, then at Commander Sisko who shook his head no. Then he turned to Captain Picard. "I know you do."

Captain Picard nodded, but said nothing as Gowron turned back to Barclay.

"vItHay', a ritual challenge, is issued by an accused against the man doing the accusing. It proves who is guilty. Or who is not. It is a fight to the death."

"B–b–but how could a fight prove innocence or guilt?" Barclay asked.

Captain Picard jumped in before Gowron could answer. "Lieutenant, Klingons believe that in mortal combat the honorable fighter, and the fighter on the side of the truth in a situation, is always victorious."

"Correct, Captain," Gowron said, beaming at Picard. "The truth will always have more strength than a lie. More inner strength. We live by such thoughts every moment. Every day."

Worf said, "He is right."

Riker glanced at Admiral Jellico, who seemed to be thinking very much about Gowron's last statement. Riker just hoped that if Gowron finally got through to the admiral, it would not be too late to make a difference.

Barclay nodded that he understood, so Gowron continued.

"The ritual chamber has a fire in the center. The combatants are dressed in ritual fighting robes. Those of us who watch form a circle. Pok and Qua'lon would fight within the circle of warriors."

Gowron took a drink, then looked again at Barclay and smiled. "I will ask you no more questions. But I must first explain the weapons of this ritual. Pok had the first choice of weapons, since his charge had been made, then denied. He chose a *bat'tLeH*. He might have picked up a knife, but Qua'lon would have beaten him easily with a *bat'tLeH*. Or he also might have chosen to fight with only his hands. A stupid choice."

Gowron took another long drink of his blood wine. "Qua'lon thought this fight to be an easy one. He did not know how much Torghn had trained his son in fighting. He did not also know how much Pok had grown inside in just the few days with seasoned warriors. The fight was very even."

Suddenly Kira's voice broke into the story. "Red alert! Commander Sisko to Ops."

Around them the lights in the bar turned to a blinking red. Everywhere Starfleet officers scrambled for the door. All at the table with Gowron remained seated for the moment.

Sisko tapped his badge as he stood. "What is happening?"

Kira's voice came back strong enough for all to hear.

"Sir," she said. "We have just had six Klingon Birds of Prey decloak. They have shields up and are in attack formation."

Almost as a unit the group stood and headed quickly for the door across an already mostly empty bar.

Behind them Riker heard Quark say, "There goes another lunch profit."

Chapter Twenty

LURSA GLANCED OVER at her sister at the weapons console. B'Etor nodded back. Good. They were in position. Now they must wait. This would be the hardest part.

She sat back and focused on the screen in front of her. The *Enterprise* had moved slightly away from the station into a more defensible position. Very smart.

Gowron's flagship and the *Botka* also moved away and had powered up its weapons.

The station had gone to full alert status and had shields up. That was the important fact. With the shields up, they could not beam Gowron off the station. If they tried she would have him again.

A simple plan. Bold.

And on Federation territory.

She laughed to herself. If the Federation lost the

head of the High Council, it would bring anger against the Federation. That anger was exactly what the House of Duras needed. A fight. A true reason to bring the Klingon Empire back to its glory.

"All ships are in position," B'Etor said. "All weapons are fully charged. Transporters stand ready."

"Good," Lursa said. "Now make sure no one moves unless I give the order."

"Done," B'Etor said a moment later. She nodded to another to take her place and moved up beside her sister. "How long will they wait?"

"I do not know," Lursa said. "But I hope not long enough for reinforcements to arrive."

B'Etor laughed. "That would be a problem," she said.

Lursa said nothing. It was the only problem with her plan. Too many reinforcements would cause her to run. But she still had something extra. She still had someone on the station.

dRacLa, son of Vok, moved along the corridor as if he were in a hurry to get to his station. The other Klingons on the Federation station would be doing the same. All would be heading to beam-out positions.

But the flashing red lights along the corridor signaled that the entire station was on red alert. No one would be beaming out. Lursa and her sister had the station under hostage. Now he had time to move.

If he knew Gowron, he would make every effort to get back to his ship. Gowron knew he could not do that from Ops. He had to go to another place. dRacLa would catch him on the way.

If Gowron did not move from Ops, dRacLa would catch him in another manner.

Either way Gowron would die. dRacLa knew he too would probably die. But killing Gowron would complete the cycle of his blood oath. An oath he had taken as a child, the day his father died.

dRacLa, son of Vok, was prepared to die.

Riker immediately studied the screen as they entered Ops. Dax and Sisko went to their stations. Gowron, Captain Picard, Worf, Admiral Jellico, and he stood above the rail.

"Report, Major," Commander Sisko said as he strolled to his position in the middle of Ops.

"Six Klingon Birds of Prey have decloaked. They have powered up full weapons and have them targeted on the station. The *Enterprise* has moved into a defensive position. Gowron's flagship and the *Botka* have also moved into defensive positions."

Sisko nodded and did a quick survey of the stations and the people he had. Riker was impressed at the man's calmness under pressure.

He finished his quick survey and faced the main screen again. "It seems we have a standoff. Have we called for help?"

"Yes, sir," Kira said. "The Hornet is six hours away. The Merrimac is ten. Gowron's ship also called for reinforcements. I estimate their arrival at eight hours."

"Lursa," Gowron said, staring at the ships on the screen. "I have underestimated that woman too many times. I did not expect this."

Sisko turned around and looked at Gowron. Riker and Captain Picard did the same.

"If you know what's going on," Sisko said. "I wish you would explain it to the rest of us."

"Yes, explain," Admiral Jellico said.

"Lursa and her sister are responsible," he said. "That much is clear. I also think they were on that other ship yesterday."

"Is this a civil war?" Sisko asked.

"No." Gowron said. He looked at Sisko. "Not yet. But I am in your house." Gowron spread his arms to take in Ops and the rest of the station. "I am in Federation territory. If I die here, your inability to protect me will be considered an insult against the Klingon Empire."

"The same as in your story," Riker said. "Torghn giving his life to save yours in his home."

"That story tells much," Gowron said.

"And we might have a full war," Picard said. "And with you dead there would be no stopping it."

"But they have no way of getting you here," Sisko said, "as long as the shields remain up. We can simply wait them out."

"If they also wait," Gowron said. "But that would be a stupid thing for Lursa to do. She is not stupid."

"Then they will attack," Picard said.

"They will attack," Gowron said. "But the question is how? Where?"

"And when," Picard said.

"And when," Gowron agreed.

Riker glanced around at Ops. Everything and everyone seemed to be in position and ready. Commander Sisko stood calmly in the center. Major Kira fidgeted at the weapons board. Dax stood calmly at the science station.

Now the question was, who moved next?

To Riker's surprise, it was Captain Picard.

Chapter Twenty-one

CAPTAIN PICARD TURNED to Gowron. "Let me see if I understand this situation correctly. If the station drops its shields, Lursa will beam everyone in Ops onto her ship, assuming one of those captured would be you."

"What?" Sisko asked, turning and moving to the rail.

Gowron nodded. "She took us once before in the same fashion. She knew I would be transporting the minute the station's shields were dropped after the meeting time. She was smart. She would know that I have come to this location now. She would take everyone in this area of the station. Kill all of us."

Picard nodded. He had figured that might be the case. It was the only factor that made sense. Lursa and her sister were gambling that either he or Gowron would attempt to transport back to their respective ships. And if Lursa and her force had to wait too long, they would pound the station until the shields dropped and then do the same thing. Again logical.

"Then we need to get you off this bridge," Sisko said. "And you too, Admiral."

"Thank you, Commander," Gowron said. "I doubt it would help the situation. There are at least twenty Klingons on the station at this moment, plus many thousands of others. I am sure Lursa has enough spies here to keep her informed as to my location." He glanced around. "I would rather stay here. Where I trust who is behind me."

Sisko smiled. "I honor your request, sir," he said.

Gowron bowed slightly in thanks.

"I will stay, also," Admiral Jellico said. "It is my place here, beside our guest."

Gowron nodded Jellico's way, a look of slight surprise on his face.

Picard also was surprised, but he did not show it. He still hadn't got the answer he was looking for. "Gowron, what would happen if we forced Lursa's hand? What if we brought in reinforcements earlier than expected?"

"She would attack the station before they arrived," Gowron said. "I am certain. She hopes to force the shields down. All her efforts will be to that end."

"Does she have the force?" Picard asked. He was familiar with the station's defenses. And with the power of the Birds of Preys, but he wanted Gowron's opinion.

"Yes." Gowron said, glancing at Commander Sisko, almost as if he was apologizing for insulting the station. "She has the power to do so in a very short period."

"What if the *Enterprise* and your two ships," Picard asked, "placed themselves between her ships and the station? Would that have an effect?"

"Six against three." Gowron smiled. "It would slow her effort considerably, if our ships could remain in positions between hers and the station. And it would cause her much damage. She does not like to lose ships. I know that much of her. Ships are her power in the Empire."

Captain Picard turned to Commander Sisko. "How far away is Gul Dukat?" Beside him Picard heard Gowron draw in a sharp breath, then snort in disgust.

Sisko turned to Major Kira. "Major?"

"They are back in Cardassian territory," she said, checking her long-range scans. Then she looked up at Commander Sisko. "They could return in forty minutes."

Sisko turned to Gowron and Picard.

"You would have Cardassians save us?" Gowron said. Picard could hear the disgust in his voice. "Yesterday was bad enough. Must I be so shamed again?"

"These Klingon ships threaten a Federation station, Gowron," Picard said. "I would call them. Not you."

"And what honor is in that?" Gowron said.

"What honor is in not defending our guests?" Picard snapped back. "In any fashion we can."

Gowron stared at Picard for a moment, then suddenly laughed. "Picard. You know us too well."

Picard nodded. He knew that with a little logic he would win that argument with Gowron. Gowron's own story had given Picard the ammunition. Now, would Gul Dukat return? That was another question again.

dRacLa had quickly discovered there was no way for one person to watch Ops without being actually in Ops. Gowron could have gone anywhere. His plan was useless. So he had immediately switched to his backup plan. He would bring the shields down himself and trust that Lursa could find Gowron, wherever the animal hid.

He moved along the corridor now toward engineering. He had studied this area of the station carefully from old Cardassian plans. He knew exactly where two timed charges would cause a cascade effect, cutting all power to shields. He had already planted one charge. He was a short twenty paces from where he need to place the second when a voice said, "Stop there."

Without an instant's hesitation, he pulled his weapon, spun, and fired.

A man in a brown-and-tan uniform stood in the middle of the corridor. Two Federation officers flanked him. Both had their weapons drawn.

dRacLa's first disrupter shot caught one guard and he went over backward.

The guard second fired his phaser, barely missing dRacLa. The man in brown simply stood still.

Quickly dRacLa dove around the corner and another phaser shot brushed his boot.

"Security," a voice behind him said. "Seal off the corridor outside engineering."

Ahead a security shield shimmered into being. Just inside where he needed to place the charge. He had failed. That much was clear. But he would not die alone.

He ducked into a dead-end side corridor and blew a hole in the lock of a door there. Quickly he went inside what appeared to be some sort of office. There was no way out. He did not expect there to be.

He leaned back out the door and fired a shot up the corridor as a warning. Then pulling out the explosive in his pack, he took the one large ball and rolled it into smaller ones. These would keep him alive awhile longer. Maybe just long enough to be rescued.

Or long enough to kill a few Federation dogs.

Then with a flick of a switch, he blew the first explosive he'd planted.

Riker watched as the comm line blinked and Major Kira studied her board. Then she looked up at Commander Sisko. "Sir. Shots have been fired in the engineering section. Odo reports they have cornered a Klingon there. He believes it to be the one whom he saw talking to the Yridian trader who set the bomb."

"dRacLa," Gowron said softly, never taking his eyes off the main screen in front of him.

Suddenly the lights blinked, then held.

"What was that?" Sisko demanded.

Without looking up from her board, Major Kira said, "There was an explosion in engineering, sir. One coupling was destroyed. No other damage."

"All energy rerouted," Dax said. "Everything is again stable."

Sisko nodded and glanced back at Captain Picard.

Riker let out the breath he was holding. That had been a close call. If the blast had taken out two power couplings, the shields would have failed for a short time. Not long, but long enough for Lursa and her sister to beam them all out of here.

"It seems it is time to act," Picard said.

Sisko nodded.

Picard tapped his comm badge. "Picard to *Enterprise.*"

"Go ahead, Captain," Data's voice came back strong.

"Send out a call to Gul Dukat. Patch it through there to me here."

"Yes, sir." Data said.

"And Data, when I am finished, move the *Enterprise* to a position between the threatening Klingon ships and the station."

"Aye, sir."

A moment later Data came back. "Go ahead, sir."

"Gul Dukat," Picard said. "Captain Picard here. I apologize for not being able to make thy request visually."

"I understand," Dukat said, "That you have a somewhat troublesome situation."

Picard smiled. "We do."

"And are you asking for my help?" Dukat said.

Riker could almost hear Dukat's voice mocking them. Just like the Cardassians. They would never make a situation easier.

Picard shook his head. He took a deep breath. "Yes, Dukat," Picard said. "I am."

"On my way," Dukat said. "Out."

Picard shook his head and turned to Gowron. "My friend, dealing with the Cardassians is difficult. For all of us."

"And very seldom worth the trouble," Gowron said.

Riker hoped this time he was wrong.

Chapter Twenty-two

LURSA ALMOST JUMPED out of the command chair. "Do these dogs have no pride? They call to Cardassians for help. They have no shame."

"The *Enterprise* is moving into a position between us and the station," B'Etor said. "And Gowron is contacting his ships. This is not as we had planned."

There was silence on the bridge for a moment, then B'Etor glanced up. "He has ordered them to do the same as the *Enterprise*. They will block us."

Lursa dropped back into the chair. An attack against the station now would be very costly. And with the Cardassians on their way, there was no more time to wait. She turned to her sister. "Are you sure of that explosion on the station?"

B'Etor nodded. "It was in the engineering section. It failed to cut the power to their shields."

Lursa nodded. dRacLa had failed, also. This day did not appear to be hers.

She turned to her sister. "There will be another day," she said.

B'Etor looked as if she was about to object, then glanced up at the main screen and nodded. "You are right, Sister. There will be another day. And I hope that day includes the death of the *Enterprise.*"

"We will work for it," Lursa said. "That much I promise." She sat back in the command chair and studied the scene one more time. Gowron's two ships were moving into a position between her and the station, flanking the *Enterprise.* Her six ships against those three. She might win quickly. But she might win slowly. There wasn't time enough to take that chance.

It was over.

"Order the ships to cloak and return home."

"Yes, Sister," B'Etor said.

"There will be another day," she said to the screen and the *Enterprise.* "There will."

"They are cloaking and going into warp," Major Kira said.

Riker could easily hear the relief and excitement in her voice. The same feeling he was experiencing. He glanced over at Dax. She looked up and returned his smile.

"They have run," Gowron said.

"It is over," Admiral Jellico said.

Riker could also hear the huge relief in the Admiral's voice. He couldn't blame him.

"No!" Gowron said. "It is not quite over. There is still a Klingon cornered like a trapped animal in your engineering section. Am I right?"

Commander Sisko turned to Major Kira, who nodded.

"It is a Klingon. I think this might be a situation best handled by my men." Gowron turned to Commander Sisko. "If I have your permission, sir?"

Sisko frowned, then nodded. "Of course."

Gowron turned to the others along the rail. "If you would like to accompany me, I will take care of this situation and then we can have our last meeting."

Admiral Jellico nodded.

Riker had no idea what Gowron had in mind. But there was no way he was going to miss it.

Twenty minutes later Riker, Commander Sisko, Captain Picard, Worf, and Admiral Jellico stood with Chancellor Gowron a safe distance down the corridor from where the Klingon was trapped. Six Federation guards crouched along one wall. Odo, Dsq's chief of security, stood in the hall near the junction.

Gowron had called for five members of his crew to beam aboard. He was now talking to one tall warrior guard.

After a moment the guard nodded, then stepped down the hall past the Federation guards as if he was walking through a safe park. Riker was amazed at his courage.

The guard got to the junction to the small dead-end corridor and stopped. "dRacLa, son of Vok," he called up the corridor. "If you are to die honorably, now is the time. I will honor your blood challenge."

Riker glanced at Picard who looked as puzzled as Riker felt. What was going on? This made no sense.

"How do I know you will not cut me down when I step forward?" A loud voice came from down the hall. Obviously the voice of the trapped Klingon.

"You have my word, as a warrior," the guard said.

Gowron leaned over to Commander Sisko and said in a moderately loud voice, "It would be good if you had your men step back out of sight."

Sisko nodded and motioned for Odo to do what Gowron suggested. The Federation officers retreated.

Riker watched as the guard at the junction opened his arms, showing someone down the hall that he had not drawn his gun.

"I could cut you down like so much meat," the unseen Klingon said.

"There would be no honor in that," the guard said. He pulled out his knife and crouched.

A moment later another Klingon lunged at him from the side hall. The guard stepped aside and the lunge missed.

Crouched, the two circled each other, making slashing motions but drawing no blood.

"dRacLa, son of Vok," Gowron said softly. "I was right."

Picard glanced at him, then nodded.

Riker had seen many fights, but for some reason this one held him spellbound. Seeing the son of a person from Gowron's story gave the fight extra meaning.

The first blood was drawn by the guard. He slashed the other's arm.

"You are good," dRacLa said, ignoring the cut on his arm.

The guard nodded, but did not respond.

They continued to circle in the small corridor, waiting, watching for the opening that would allow the other to make the fatal thrust.

It did not take long. dRacLa lunged at what he saw as an opening.

The guard moved aside, very light on his feet for such a large man. Then he caught dRacLa with an upward thrust. The knife went in solidly and Riker could hear dRacLa's breath burst from him.

The guard held him there, suspended on his knife for a moment, then pulled the knife out suddenly.

dRacLa slumped to the ground. With only a glance up at the guard standing over him, he died.

Gowron nodded. "Now, it is finished." He moved down the hall and slapped the guard on the back.

The other Klingons did the same. They all ignored the body on the floor.

The guard returned his knife to his belt, and Gowron, his arm around the shoulder of the guard, came back down the hall. Riker could not remember ever seeing such a happy, almost fatherly proud smile on Gowron's face.

Then, as if by a sudden bolt, Riker understood.

"My friends," Gowron said. "I am now proud to say that my long story has a finish. Admiral Jellico. Commander Sisko. Captain Picard. Commander Riker. Lieutenant Worf. This is Pok, son of Torghn. My first officer."

Captain Picard stuck out his hand, smiling. "I am honored."

And as far as Riker was concerned, the captain spoke for all of them.

Epilogue

DINNER.

The meal in Quark's had been superb. Now they sipped their brandy and relaxed. Around them the normal nightly activity of Quark's had come up to full speed. But somehow it seemed to avoid their table, as if they were sitting in their own private bubble.

Riker wasn't exactly sure why the meal had tasted so good. Possibly because he and Dax were finally allowed to finish a meal together. Or more likely it had been her company. And her laughs. He loved it when she laughed.

And when she smiled.

And when she just looked at him.

Just a plain enjoyable meal. In fact, at the moment he could not remember a meal being so enjoyable. Tender roast Jibetian duckling. Crisp young sprouts.

The finest of Quark's brandy. He held the memory of the flavors like a treasured gem. He would not soon let go of them.

"You are just sitting there smiling," Dax said. "A personal joke? Or a private thought?"

"It's you," Riker said, leaning forward to get a little closer to her. "For some reason you make me smile."

"Thank you, kind sir," she said, raising her glass. They toasted each other and he sipped his brandy again, letting the smooth, smoky flavor coat his mouth.

"I hear you volunteered to help set up the holodeck program, Dax said. "Is that true?"

"Very true," Riker said. "And I'm looking forward to it."

That afternoon, at the last meeting, Captain Picard had suggested that Gowron's story of Pok be used as a Federation holodeck program to teach Federation personnel about Klingon customs and culture.

Gowron had loved the idea. No hesitations.

But Admiral Jellico had been a tougher sell. Finally Gowron had offered to be scanned for inclusion in this program and that had swung the admiral. It would be a very worthwhile project. Of that, Riker had no doubt.

"Well," Dax said, glancing over her glass of brandy at Riker. "What would you like to do now, Commander? It seems we have some time free."

Riker smiled at her devil-may-care look. Just at that moment a cheer exploded from the Dabo table. He glanced that way, then looked back at her. He could feel the intense grin on his face, and for some reason he had no desire to tone it down.

"First off," he said. "I would love to play Dabo. I have a feeling I just might break Quark's bank."

Dax raised her eyebrows. "You must really feel lucky tonight."

He reached across the table and took her hand. Then, smiling, he asked, "Don't you?"

THE MAKING OF
STAR TREK: KLINGON!
by
David Mack

Introduction

The choice of the irascible but always highly honorable warrior race known as the Klingons to be the stars of the latest innovation in CD-ROM entertainment from Simon and Schuster Interactive was no accident, no simple coincidence.

Ever since their first TV appearance in the 1960s original series episode, "Errand of Mercy," the Klingons have captivated the imaginations of *Star Trek* fans everywhere. They returned in such memorable episodes as "The Trouble with Tribbles" and "Day of the Dove," among others, and were the first denizens of the *Star Trek* universe to greet fans at the beginning of the series' big-screen debut, *Star Trek: The Motion Picture*.

The Klingons took on true depth during the phenomenally successful seven-year run of *Star Trek: The Next Generation,* fueled by the overwhelming popularity of Michael Dorn's Lieutenant Worf. With a Klingon protagonist as a regular character, fans were at long last treated to an up-close and personal look at the rituals and traditions of the Klingon people. And with Dorn's Worf keeping the Klingon mystique going strong on *Star Trek: Deep Space Nine* and Roxann Biggs-Dawson's half-Klingon engineer, B'Elanna Torres, carrying the torch on *Star Trek: Voyager,* it's a sure bet that the legend of the Klingons is just getting started.

So, having spread their Empire through the Alpha Quadrant, four television series, and six of the seven *Star Trek* films as well as countless comic books and novels, the Klingons now have conquered the newest media frontier—the interactive CD-ROM.

The creation of an interactive CD-ROM, particularly one as sophisticated and revolutionary as the *Star Trek: Klingon!* CD-ROM, is no easy task. It involves the coordinated effort of a great many people working together for many months, and sometimes years, to produce the final product; the best way to understand the origins and history of the *Klingon!* CD-ROM is to hear it in the words of the people who made it happen.

Preproduction

Like all great accomplishments, the *Klingon!* CD-ROM was born from an idea. And the author of that idea was its executive producer, Keith Halper.

"The idea came out in a title meeting that we had nearly two years ago," Halper recalled. "We wanted to create a suitable follow-up to the *Star Trek: The Next Generation: Interactive Technical Manual* (Simon and Schuster Interactive's best-selling "virtual tour" of the *Starship Enterprise 1701-D,* which Halper also produced). To match the success of the *Interactive Technical Manual,* this new CD-ROM would have to be authentic and visually rivetting, and take the medium to bold new places. That's what *Star Trek* fans demand. Unlike the technical manual, however, we wanted this CD-ROM to use characters and plot and high action: We wanted it to have the feel of an interactive television episode.

"When we did the *Interactive Technical Manual,* one of the things we learned was that an interactive product allows us to explore in detail things which can be presented only superficially in a linear format," Halper explained. "For example, when we see Picard's quarters in an episode, we see it for maybe ten seconds and it just flashes by. There's a lot of detail in that room. The books on the shelves were chosen with care. We know that Picard reads the British empiricists and the German rationalists, like

Kant. That's the kind of stuff you can't see in an episode, but it adds to the flavor of the room. In an interactive product we allow you to wander around and explore the space and learn more about these people and see some of the more subtle details, maybe learn something new about them that wouldn't have been possible in another way.

It was obvious to me that "this story have to be about the Klingons. When we first saw the Klingons, we got to know them only superficially. They were this violent, aggressive, warlike species, and there's really nothing very good about them. That's pretty much all we ever saw of them in the original series. . . . During *Star Trek: The Next Generation* we came to know a lot more about them. Through Worf, we get to see that they're actually this noble, honorable race, and that their warlike tendencies actually have a logical basis and form the root of their culture. But that's the kind of stuff that we learn only over time and upon examination.

"We thought that in an interactive product, we could again allow users to do something analogous to wandering around the rooms—that we could allow users to wander around in their culture, to understand the books that are on their cultural shelves, and to understand who they are in a more profound way.

"So, for instance, when you're wandering around in the living room and stop and click on a statue, and the Klingon computer voice talks with reverence about the intertwining circles of the fulfilled and unfulfilled blood oaths on the statue, the blood-oath circles, that's really interesting and that says something kind of profound about the Klingons that you haven't seen in an episode. There isn't time in an episode to go into this kind of detail. In an interactive program, we can put tons of detail in there and allow users to poke around and find it and teach themselves."

With the focus set firmly on Klingons, the next step in the genesis of the Klingon-themed CD-ROM was to develop a story that would form the core of a complete "Klingon-immersion experience." And after that would come a teleplay—one unlike any written before.

"Liz Braswell, my associate editor, and I conceived originally of a sort of Hamlet-like story in which there were two brothers who were fighting over a kingdom," Halper said. "One of the brothers is killed and then his son avenges him. Of course, we know that a Klingon Hamlet wouldn't be troubled by all kinds of indecision like a human Hamlet.

"Keith . . . got the idea and I helped write one of the original scripts for it when we were still trying to decide how to do this 'choose-your-own-adventure' style of computer game," Braswell added. "There were several evenings where we were on our hands and knees, writing up dialogue, cutting and pasting it on on the floor to show where different story threads went."

From that spark the torch was lit and passed to the husband-and-wife writing partnership of Kristine Katherine Rusch and Dean Wesley Smith. Rusch is the author of more than twenty novels and currently serves as editor of the renowned *Magazine of Fantasy and Science Fiction*. She received the 1994 Hugo Award winner for Best Professional Editor for her work at *F&SF*. Smith has authored fourteen novels and numerous short stories, and was the winner of the World Fantasy Award in 1989.

"We did the story that inspired the script, and now we are doing a novelization of the script, in which Gowron initially tells the story of Pok in Quark's bar," Smith said. "From that telling, the Federation decides to set up the holodeck program, and Gowron agrees to take part."

Rusch and Smith's story was only the first step in a long process of rewriting that would continue even during production.

"Essentially, we handed Hilary Bader this big pile of storylines and outlines and sketches and said, 'Oh, by the way, Hilary, we need a script in three weeks because we have to start building sets,'" Halper remembered with a grin. "And Hilary really rose to the task. Hilary's wonderful. She's done probably a half-dozen episodes of the various *Star Treks*. She was recommended to me by Suzie Domnick of Paramount Licensing: She was experienced and could come through in a pinch. And Hilary did come through."

"The writing was unusually rushed," Bader recalled. "There wasn't a lot of time for endless rewriting. I wrote the first draft, which went to Ron Moore [Ronald D. Moore, *Deep Space Nine* producer and *Star Trek Generations* scriptwriter] for comments. Ron came in with a lot of ideas for changes. Unfortunately I didn't have a lot of time to implement them. I knew I couldn't have a second draft done by the first day of shooting without rushing through it and I didn't want to do that. So I made sure Director Jonathan Frakes had the first two days' worth of script before the shooting began, then I was able to finish the rewrites on the rest of the script while they were shooting the first few days.

"Because there are always problems with a script that don't become obvious until you are shooting it, I was on the set the entire time," Bader added. "If there was a problem, something I wrote couldn't be shot a certain way, or Jonathan Frakes wanted to include some character in the scene who wasn't written in, he'd ask for an on-the-spot rewrite.

"I have to say, the two weeks of shooting was the most fun I've ever had in Hollywood," Bader confided. "I felt much closer to this project than I have to anything else I've ever written."

"Hilary has a natural affinity for interactive script-writing," Halper said with genuine admiration. "She developed a scripting format—because one didn't exist—which we undoubtedly will use on future projects. It really worked, because it was something that told our programmers what they needed to know, and at the same time it looks a lot like a film script. Now, we're going through a traditional production process, so we needed something that [the production crew] knew how to work with. We didn't want to surprise the guy doing opticals or the people setting up lighting. They need to look at a script and say, 'Well, it doesn't really hang together because the scenes don't read chronologically, but I can follow these instructions.' And I thought it was just brilliant.

"In addition to that," Halper continued, "Hilary has a very light touch; she's very funny and she breathed life into these characters. I can't credit her enough; I think that she did a lot in a very critical situation."

But while the writers and producers toiled over the glamorous task of penning the script, the project's technical experts and developers were being coordinated by associate producer Elizabeth Braswell. There was a *Language Lab* CD-ROM to be developed and new technologies to be explored before this ground-breaking endeavor could begin production.

At the top of the list for new technology was the Duck Corp.'s innovative offering, *TrueMotion,* the latest advance in full-screen, full-motion video, which Duck's Stan Marder describes as "a set of algorithms to compress video and audio where the resulting playback equals or exceeds what the average consumer sees on television. . . . Except it has the digital attributes so that you can, for instance, 'branch' the video, which you can't do any other way, and you can add all kinds of functionality to make the video itself totally interactive."

Duck also developed another new technology in tandem with *TrueMotion,* called *comprending.* "It's an amalgam of two words, and it means 'compression rendering,'" Marder explained. "What it allows you to do is real-time compositing on the fly. What we bring to the table is the ability for the end user to manipulate the comprended image on his own."

Marder offered an example of what that means: "In the movie *Forrest Gump,* when Tom Hanks goes over and shakes hands with Kennedy, we know that didn't really happen. When we watch this, we sit passively and watch that happen. We don't control Tom Hanks's movement. Comprending allows a developer to create in his program the ability to control the actors, control what is happening on the screen—in other words, move video around independently.

"So what we allow the developer to do is create a video and then manipulate that video over other video. It's a very powerful technology in the right hands. You can do amazing things with it." Comprending also allows "hot zones"—layers of digital information that will prompt a response on the screen from the "video sprite" cursor to alert users that there are data to be found.

Another scientific advance critical to the *Klingon!* CD-ROM was the development of a speech-recognition system that would be able to help teach users to speak Klingon—which is a far more daunting proposal than it might sound. For that, Simon and Schuster Interactive looked to Dragon Systems, one of the world's leading developers of voice-recognition software, and its resident Klingon-language specialist, Mark Mandel.

"When Liz and Keith were looking for people to do the speech recognition for the *Klingon!* CD project," Mandel said, "Shawn True, who is adminstratively in charge of this end of the project here at Dragon, told me that when he was asked by Liz if we would be interested in that, and he was able to answer offhandedly that we had a major Klingon linguist on our staff, he could hear her jaw hit the floor.

"As it happens, I am a linguist—a language scientist—and a science-fiction fan. And I've been studying and playing with the Klingon language for about three years or so. So I got a great kick out of it."

Armed with cutting-edge science and their own enthusiasm, Mandel and his colleagues took on the Herculean task of developing the core software of the *Klingon!* CD's *Language Lab.* "This wasn't just a Klingon recognizer we were developing," Mandel explained. "The purpose of a normal recognizer is to take speech input to direct some activity or to put a word on the screen and eventually on paper or fax or whatever. . . . The Klingon system had things turned around because our mandate for this system was to create a pronunciation tester. Every time you say a word, it knows what word you're supposed to be saying. And the objective is to correct your pronunciation.

"So that meant we knew the word you were trying to say. But I had to figure out how to detect mispronunciations—and, furthermore, do so in an intelligent way. We'd never been faced with that sort of an issue before and we did not have the time of the resources—either in terms of money, personnel, or native speakers—to do this the proper way. . . . What we did was try to anticipate ways people might mispronounce a word. So what we did was record various kinds of anticipated mispronunciations, along with the correct pronunciations. So our speakers had to produce not only correct Klingon pronunciations, but also mispronunciations, things that they've spent years learning how *not* to do. And as the experienced Klingon speakers told me after their recording sessions, that was the hardest part—getting the *mispronunciations* right."

The inclusion of the *Language Lab* CD-ROM obviously was motivated by the undeniable popularity of the Klingon language itself. "The [Klingon] language is so beautifully designed that it's actually fairly simple to learn," Braswell commented when asked what made this faux-alien tongue such a hit with fans. "There aren't twelve different cases or tenses. It's a very logically constructed language, because it was created artificially instead of organically. It's like when you're a kid, and you make up a secret code to speak with your friends. Well, Klingon is like a bigger version of that code, where you know that only other people who like the same thing you do"—in other words, *Star Trek*—"speak this language. I also think there's the 'Oh my God, this is so cool, this is a totally made-up language!' factor to consider."

And what is Klingon's appeal for linguists? "Natural languages generally have a certain degree of symmetry in their sound structures. Klingon's is twisted. It's warped. Distorted. Marc Okrand [the linguist who created the Klingon language] had a lot of fun building it," Mandel remarked humorously.

Production

With preproduction completed—except for the script, which would continue to undergo revision during shooting—and the technological foundation firmly in place, producers Halper and Braswell entrusted the reins to director Jonathan Frakes.

Frakes, best known as Commander William Riker of *Star Trek: The Next Generation,* also is an experienced director, and one whom the producers felt was the logical choice for this ambitious foray into interactive media. Frakes's decision to direct the product was motivated by two simple factors: curiosity and opportunity.

"It was something new I'd never done before. I was offered the job, and that was it," Frakes quipped.

Robert O'Reilly reprised the role of Gowron, leader of the Klingon High Council, which he created in numerous appearances on *Star Trek: The Next Generation,* and production commenced.

Frakes soon found that directing an interactive CD-ROM differed in many ways from directing for film or television. "There's no 'coverage,' which means you have to do the point of view in a continuous shot," he said. "It's linear, as opposed to shooting a master shot and then cutting in for close-ups, which is confusing to a player. So you have to design shots that don't cut. You don't want to break the flow. We fell out of that a couple of times and took some dramatic license, but as a whole, that point of view needed to be maintained through the whole game. It was tough."

A testament to Frakes's uniquely well-suited talent for directing interactive products was that he realized that the new medium would have its own technical considerations as well as logistical needs.

"I had to go to Tokyo over the summer," recalled Duck Corps' Marder. "While I was in Tokyo I checked in with my office and found I got a call from Keith [Halper]. I called Keith from Tokyo and he told me that Jonathan Frakes wanted to know if I could send one of my engineers to Paramount to be there when they set up their lighting and start the shooting process so that Jonathan could get some test compression done on the soundstage, so that he could see what final results were going to be."

"We were concerned about the lighting," Frakes explained, "because Klingons' costumes are dark, their sets are dark, and the feel of them is dark. We were afraid because a lot of CD-ROMs look dark anyway. And we were right, we had to use brighter light. Later it was transferred and compressed down to a color we liked."

"This was the first time that I've had a director say that's what he wants to do," Marder said admiringly of Frakes. "And it was so important, because he realized this wasn't going to be seen on television, it wasn't going to be in a movie theater, it's a new medium."

Although Frakes found directing interactive to be different from his work in film and TV, actor O'Reilly felt right at home in the new medium. "It's really not that different," the actor confessed. "It really doesn't make that much of a difference to an actor. I've even filmed different endings to TV shows or films. It happens in our business. It happened even before the CD-ROM came on the scene. Producers might not like an ending or they might feel unsure of an ending so they'll film it twice. It's a rarity but it does occur. In television and film you really have to learn how to turn on a dime with what's going on, so CD-ROM is nothing unusual. You've got three or four different answers and you know you have to do the work, so it's just like life. You do it."

Even once shooting had started, the merry chaos was far from over. Many of those who were on the soundstage have vivid memories of the more absurd moments.

"There was one day of shooting when we had a crew come in from *Entertainment Tonight,* and they were shooting during lunch hour," Halper divulged conspiratorially. "Since they were shooting during lunch hour, we kept the soundstage doors shut. Now, what happens when you're using smoke and have lights on all day is the temperature in the place goes way up, and you open up the doors during lunch to cool the place down. Well, we never did that. So when they came in the afternoon, it had to have been 115 degrees in there. And then it kept getting hotter and hotter and hotter, and there was poor Robert O'Reilly with his Klingon mask melting right off of his face."

O'Reilly and his fellow Klingons enjoyed their share of laughs as well over at the Paramount Commissary. "You get a lot of looks," he said matter-offactly. "Certainly, when you walk down the street, eyes turn, and there was one time when we were filming for the CD-ROM, we were walking by and some Paramount executives had some people from the network affiliates as guests. And they were fascinated by it, because most of them had never seen Klingons up close, and there were about six of us. And it's unusual to see that many Klingons at once, anyway, except in a dream, and I'm not sure if that would be a good dream."

Perhaps the most memorable moment during the filming of the *Klingon!* CD-ROM was the inaugural performance of the Klingon National Anthem.

"There's just something wonderfully absurd about working with a room full of Klingons, aside from the olfactory pleasure," Frakes joked. "The night that we constructed the Klingon National Anthem, [the Klingons] rising to sing on the bridge of the warbird, is a night that we will all remember for a long time. Complete, total absurdity. . . . I think it's the high point of the piece."

"Magic," was how Halper described the moment that the anthem became reality. "All the Klingons are sitting on the bridge of the Bird of Prey and they've just . . . found a big clue on their great quest. So now they feel like they're not wandering around aimlessly, but instead they have a purpose. There's nothing more stirring than a Klingon with a purpose, so all of a sudden, Gowron beats his hands against his chair— *Bam! Bam! Bam!*—and then the gunner stands up, because she knows the song that he's beating the time to—it's the Klingon National Anthem. And she begins to sing this very moving song—*'HoY, Kahless PuKLod. . . . '*—and everybody jumps in. . . . I felt like I had participated in *Star Trek* history at that moment.

"The way that was written was that Hilary wrote something in English, then she faxed it out to Marc Okrand," Halper continued. "Then Okrand translated it to Klingon and put his literal translation below the Klingon verses. The literal translation is always skewed at bit, so if you send him 'Row, row, row your boat,' you'll get back 'Propel, propel, propel your craft.' "

Bader recalled her own slice of surrealism from the two-week shoot. "During much of the shoot, there were a few actors who were in almost every day," she said. "The poor actors, Kahless bless them, would come in at some horrendous hour, like around four A.M., and get Klingonized. By the time I arrived at a reasonable eight or nine A.M., there was a studio filled with nothing but Klingons.

"During the filming of any movie, there is a lot of downtime for the actors. One of the actors, his name was Paul, would come over and hang with us. After two weeks of long days, I got to be quite friendly with him.

"One day we were staying late to shoot some scene involving only one actor, probably Robert [O'Reilly]. The other actors were released to costuming and makeup to be de-Klingonized. As we're shooting, this nice-looking guy comes up to me and starts talking to me. As if he knows me. Very friendly, very chummy. I thought, 'Who the heck is this guy?' I was growing uncomfortable.

"Finally—he must have sensed my discomfort— he said to me, 'You don't know who I am, do you? I'm Paul.' I was shocked. This was my Klingon bud. The guy I'd spent the last two weeks with for hours every day, and I didn't recognize him. In fact, even after he told me who he was I still felt weird talking to him."

Postproduction

By the time shooting was finished, the final phase of the *Klingon!* CD-ROM already was well under way Like a film or TV episode, the CD-ROM needed to be edited and its various software components assembled in their proper sequence.

Being a producer of interactive CD-ROM is "somewhat similar to being a television producer," Halper said, "with the one caveat that you have this whole other element TV producers don't have to worry about, which is programming. And the people who are programming have as much creative input as anybody else in the process."

"Once the raw Klingon CD footage was shot, Keith passed it all—all this video, all this music, all this audio—into my hands to finish up the technological side," Braswell remarked. "I act as the contact with the developers—Dragon Systems and Touchscreen— and I make sure this project goes from being just video to being not just a game, but a true interactive experience."

The edited and enhanced video and audio materials from the production team at Paramount, the speech-recognition protocols from Dragon Systems, and the *TrueMotion* software from Duck Corp. were then delivered to the technical wizards at Touchscreen, who assembled it into a digital product. The step-by-step process of how that transpires was provided by Touchscreen's Cheryl Meollenbeck.

"The traditional media gets delivered to us in some kind of videotape format, DAT tape format, or audio-CD-type format," Meollenbeck explained. "We receive all of the media from whoever has done pieces of this project, digitize it, or we compress it—if it's video footage it gets both digitized and compressed—and then we take care of all the synching-up of the audio to the video in a digital format. And that would be media preparation—converting all the assets into a digital format.

"Once they're in that format," Meollenbeck continued, "we have to have a staff of **programmers** work to build an 'engine.' For *Star Trek: Klingon!* there were two engines needed—one to support the interactive episode, and the other one was a gaming engine to support the *Language Lab*.

"My partner, Dennis McCole, has a strong television background," Meollenbeck added. "He was the technical director on the shoot, working with Jonathan Frakes to ensure that the point-of-view perspective was portrayed properly, that from a user-interaction standpoint the scenes would work. Jona than's kind of a traditional film director, but this product was shot in full point of view, which is not a typical way to shoot a film. So adherence to the core design was our responsibility—during preproduction, throughout the shooting, and again in postproduction."

Once the early working prototypes were delivered to Simon and Schuster Interactive by Touchscreen executive producer Halper paused to reflect on the nearly two years he had devoted to bringing this project to fruition, and the roles various people played in making it happen.

"I was showing the beta version off at the Paramount lot, and a lot of people were very surprised that we were able to do something like this on a comput er," Halper said proudly. "I am really appreciative of the work that Duck did. They have something which is truly revolutionary"

But while Halper was pleased with the final result of his labors, he mused that the personal cost was higher than he had expected. "I was on the Paramount lot for the whole prep, the shoot, and all of the editing," he said. "I got involved in this to a degree that I don t want to repeat. At one point I was listening to all the sound effects and evaluating the Foley and saying, 'Oh, no, so-and-so's footsteps would be much heavier than that.' I've been told that Rick Berman gets involved like this, gets his hands in every single detail because he feels it's critical to ensuring the quality of his show. . . . It's inspirational."

"Inspirational" is a word that might be applied to the reason for all this work and invention, the Klingons themselves. Undoubtedly, their popularity motivated the *Klingon!* CD-ROM's genesis, and its creators are hopeful that it also will spur the three-CD-ROM set on to record sales. But what do the people behind its creation think makes these ridgepated, easily provoked disciples of honor so popular with the fans?

"They're a cultural archetype," Braswell offered as a possible explanation. "They're the Vikings, the samurai, the Native Americans. They're a pure warrior society, the likes of which America hasn't ever really known. We may be striving toward that *Star Trek: The Next Generation* sort of peaceful coexistence, but there is something in us all which really longs for simple, pure animal release, the spartan lifestyle, the notion that honor is what's important, not remembering to set your VCR to tape *Frasier* or get your taxes done on time. Klingons represent a simpler way of being which we don't have now.

"And in Klingon society if you don't like your boss you challenge him to a duel," Braswell remarked wistfully. "If you kill him, you get to take his job, which is the American dream."

"Klingons, ya gotta love 'em. . . . Because if you don't, they'll kill you," Bader quipped. "Seriously? I feel like it's not for me to say. I love them. The fact that honor is what drives them, yet they keep room in their lives for art, poetry, song."

"They smell. As a breed, they stink," Frakes declared without hesitation. "But they have a primal connection. They are warriors, they are direct, they don't seem to work with much of a hidden agenda. And they wear turtles on their heads."

"Because they're sort of straight-on people and they're uncomplicated," O'Reilly said with the conviction of one who knows. "They have honor, which they prize above all else, and I think that's what humans really want more than anything else, but we get a little bit convoluted in our lives. . . . Everything is either right or wrong for them. . . . In some ways, they're almost like the knights of King Arthur's court before the fall. Plus, they know how to have fun."

And in the end equation, fun is what it's all about. *Qapla'*.

They Came from Beyone Time and Space . . .
Who Would Be Bold Enough to
Stand Against Them?

This June, The Invasion Begins!

BOOK ONE

First Strike!

by

Diane Carey

"They will not go off, Captain," Kellen said. "You have no choice now. You will have to fight with them."

"We'll see about that. Mister Sulu, ahead one-half impulse. Mister Chekov, take the science station. Ensign Donnier, take navigations."

The assistant engineer blinked in surprise, then dropped to the command deck. Chekov jumped up to Spock's library computer and science station. Donnier slipped into Chekov's vacant seat and barely settled all the way down. He was a competent assistant for Scott, but he'd never been on the bridge before. He was young and particularly good-looking, which got him in many doors, only there to stumble over his personal insecurity because of a stuttering problem that he let slow him down. He'd requested duty only in engineering. That was why Kirk had ordered him to put in time on the bridge.

The unidentified ship began to return fire—one, two, three globular bulbs of energy that looked more than anything like big blue water balloons wobbling through space toward the Klingon cruiser. Two missed, but one hit and drenched the cruiser in crackling blue, green, and white destructive power. The cruiser wasn't blown up, but fell off and spun out of control.

"Heavy damage to the cruiser, sir," Chekov reported. "Main engines are seizing."

"Analyze those bolts."

"Analyzing," Spock's baritone voice answered from up on that monitor.

Kirk glanced up there. He'd been talking to Chekov.

He returned his attention to the main screen, where the remaining four Klingon ships were dodging those heavy blue globes and pummeling the unidentified ship so unbrokenly that Kirk winced in empathy. "Stand by photon torpedoes."

"Photon torpedoes ready," Donnier struggled, barely audibly.

As if he were standing at Kirk's side, Spock read off his analysis. "The unidentified ship's salvos are composed of quadra-cobalt intrivium . . . phased incendiary corosite plasma . . . and I believe, plutonium. They also seem to have some wrecking qualities based on sonics."

"Everything's in there," Kirk muttered. "Fusion, phasers, fire, sound . . . effective, but not supernatural. Double shields shipwide."

"Double shields, sir."

"They will use their mass-dropping weapon if you give them the chance, Kirk," Kellen rumbled. "They can negate the gravity in the whole sector. You must attack them before they use it."

"If they have that kind of technology, General, then we're already sunk," Kirk responded, watching the action. "And they don't seem to have it."

"How can you know?"

"Because your ships are getting in some good punches and the visitors haven't used that 'weapon' again. They're using conventional defenses. If they have hand grenades, why are they shooting with bows and arrows? Helm, full impulse."

"Full impulse, sir."

"Good," Kellen whispered, then aloud said again, "Good. Fight them with this monster of yours, while we have the advantage."

"Just keep back," Kirk warned. "Helm, come to three-four-nine. Get between those Klingon ships. Force them to break formation."

"Kirk!" Kellen pressed forward and the guards had to grab him again.

Around them the giant *Artemis* hummed as she powered up to her full potential and all her systems came on-line. A choral song of heat and imagination, she took a deep bite into space and moved in on the clutch of other ships, cleaving them away from each other with the sheer force of her presence and her sprawling shields.

Two of the Klingon ships were pressured to part formation, while one other was forced off course and had to vector around again, which took time.

In his mind Kirk saw his starship plunge into the battle. He'd put her through hell in their time together and she'd always come out with her spine uncracked. She'd picked herself up, given a good shake, and brought him and his crew back in under her own power every time. This was one of those moments when he felt that esprit with sailors from centuries past, who understood what a ship really was, how a bolted pile of wood, metal, and motive power could somehow be alive and command devotion as if the heart of oak actually pumped blood. How fast? How strong? How much could she take? How tightly could she twist against the pressure of forces from outside and inside? How far could they push her before she started to buckle? How much of herself would she give up before she let her crew be taken? How *tough* was she?

Those were the real questions, because the ship was their lives. If she died, they died. When a ship is life, it becomes alive.

"Port your helm, Mister Sulu, wear ship," he said. "Mister Donnier, phasers one-half power and open fire."

"Wear the ship, aye," Sulu said, at the same time as Donnier responded, "One half phasers, sir."

Firing bright orange streamers, the starship came about, her stern section and main hull pivoting as if the engineering hull were held on a string high above.

Kirk gripped his own chair with one hand and Donnier's chair back with the other. "Ten points more to port."

"Ten points, sir."

"Good . . . twenty points more . . . keep firing, Mister Donnier."

The ship swung about, showing them a moving

panorama of stars and ships on the main screen, swinging almost lazily from right to left.

When he couldn't see the unidentified ship on the main screen anymore, he said, "Midships."

"Midships," Sulu said, and tilted his shoulders as he fought to equalize the helm.

Donnier glanced at Kirk, plainly confused by the term *midships* on something other than a docking maneuver. Good thing Sulu was at the helm instead of someone with less experience. Maneuvering a ship at sublight speeds, in tight quarters, had entirely different characteristics than maneuvers, even battles, at warp.

At warp speed, the helm maneuvers were very slight and specific, designated by numbers of mark and course, and even moving the "wheel" a pin or two had the sweeping results of millions of light-years.

But at impulse speed, things changed. And changed even more in tight-maneuvering conditions. Helm adjustments became more sweeping, bigger, sometimes a full 180 degrees, or any cut of the pie. *Midships* meant "find the navigational center of this series of movements and equalize the helm."

Forcing her crew to lean, the starship dipped briefly to port, then surged and came about to her own gravitational center and ran her phasers across the hulls of the *Qul* and the *MatHa'*, knocking them out of their attack formation. The point of Donnier's tongue was sticking out the corner of his mouth, and his backside was hitched to the edge of his seat as he concentrated on his phasers, following not the angle of his phaser bolts but the position of the moving Klingon ships out there—it was exactly the right thing to do. Like pointing a finger.

The two Klingon ships wobbled, shivered, nearly collided, and bore off, one of them forced astern and down. Kirk hoped Kellen took note that the starship's punches were being pulled.

"Good shooting, Mister Donnier," he offered. "Maintain."

Sweating, Donnier mouthed an aye, aye, but there was no sound to it.

The other two cruisers—he forgot their names—kept wits and plowed in again, opening fire now on the *Enterprise*. The ship rocked and Kirk had to grab his command chair to keep from slamming sideways into the rail. His scratched fingers burned with the effort.

Full phasers.

He didn't want to respond in kind. He wanted to make a point, not chop four other ships to bits.

Well, not yet.

The problem was that their commanding general was here, out of communication. They might take that as final orders and fight to the death.

Qul was back in the fight now, firing on the unidentified ship, and Donnier was doing an admirable job of detonating the Klingon phaser bolts before they struck the giant fan blades. He managed to catch three out of four bolts. Not bad.

Kirk pulled himself around the helm against the heel of the starship. "Keep it up, Mister Donnier. Photon torpedoes on the Klingon vessels, Mister Sulu. Fire across their bows and detonate at proximity."

"Aye, sir."

New salvos spewed from the *Enterprise*, making a spitting sound here within the bridge, much different from the screaming streamers of phaser fire, much more concentrated and heavy-punching, exploding right in front of the *Qul*. The *Qul* flinched, probably blinded by the nearby explosions, and bore off on a wingtip, forced to cease fire and try to come about again.

"Call them off, Kellen," Kirk said. "I'll open up on them if I have to."

"What right have you to do that?" Kellen bellowed. "I brought you here to be my ally!"

"But I'm not going to be your mercenary. Call them off."

But Kellen only glared at the screen and clamped his mouth shut.

"Fine," Kirk grumbled.

As the firing intensified, the fans on the unidentified ship's long twisted hull began to close inward, lying tightly and protectively upon each other and creating a shell instead of a flower. The curve of the hull itself began to straighten out, like a snake uncoiling its body, thinning the field of target and making it harder to hit. Talk about looking like a living thing . . .

The strange ship continued to fire those sickly blue globes on the Klingon vessels that strafed it.

"All right, General, have it your way," Kirk ground out. "Mister Donnier, phasers on full power. Mister Sulu, photon torpedoes full intensity, point-blank range. Fire as your weapons bear on any Klingon vessel."

Kellen cranked around against the guard's hold on him and glared at Kirk. "No!"

"It's your decision." Kirk met the glare with his burning eyes. "Call them off!"

The Klingon's lips parted, peeled back, then came together again in a gust of frustration. He all but stomped his foot. Yanking one arm away from the guard on his left, he reached for his communicator, still being held by the other guard. As if it were all part of the same order, the guard let him have it.

Kellen snapped the communicator open and barked, *"Qul! Mev! YIchu'Ha."*

Short and sweet.

Worked, though.

The Klingon vessels swung about, joined each other at a notable distance, then dropped speed and came to a stop in some kind of formation Kirk hadn't seen before. Good enough.

"You seem to have the ear of your squadron, General," Kirk said. "Mister Donnier, cease fire. Helm, minimum safe distance, then come about and all stop."

"Aye, sir," Sulu said tightly.

"Safe distance," Kellen protested, shaking his big head. "Warriors coming home shredded and shamed, spewing tales of a Federation devil with hands of fire and steel in his eyes. 'I fought Kirk! My honor is not so damaged as if I fought a lesser enemy!' It's become an acceptable excuse to lose to Kirk. Some want to avoid you, some want to challenge you because it would be a better victory. I expected you to come in and shake planets. And *this* is you? Talk? I wanted a warrior. All I find is this—you—who will not act. I will go home and slap my commanders who spoke of you."

"Your choice," Kirk said, ruffled less than he would have anticipated at the Klingon's lopsided insults that actually were kind of complimentary. Matching the general's anger with his own control, he countered, "When you met them before, did you try to talk to them at all?"

"No!"

"So you opened fire without announcement."

"They kidnapped me. My fleet came in and took me back. Of course we fired. I brought you to fight them, not defend them."

"You brought me here to handle the situation. So let me handle it."

"I am disappointed in you, Kirk," the general said. "You do not deserve to be Kirk!"

"That's your problem." With a bob of his brows, Kirk raised his voice just enough. For a moment he gazed at the alien ship, then cast Kellen a generous glance. "Be patient. Mister Sulu, move us in again. Let's see if they'll talk to us."

"Witness you conquerors . . . we the grand unclean, languishers in eternal transience, come now from the depths of evermore. Persistent . . . we have kept supple, fluid, and . . . changeable . . . because we were destined to return. You have . . . cowered through the eons, knowing this day would come. . . . It has come. Because we are forgiving, we shall give you the opportunity to leave this . . . sector . . . or you will be cast away as we were cast away . . . or you will be destroyed as you have done to us. With your last moments you will know justice. We are . . . the impending. Now gather all you own, gather your kin . . . and stand aside."

The message thrummed and boomed through the low rafters of the bridge, then echoed into silence. No ending, just silence. Waiting.

Everyone held still, and watched the captain.

The sound of the heavy, eerie, haunted-house voice remained in every mind, and spoke over and over. *Stand aside . . .*

Tightening and untightening his aching arm, aware of McCoy watching him because he'd never reported to sickbay for his own treatment, Kirk indulged in a scowl and tipped his head to Uhura. "Lieutenant, what's the problem with that translator?"

"I don't know, sir," she said, playing her board. "Having some trouble distilling the accurate meaning of some of their words and phrases."

"Fix it. I don't want to have to guess."

"Trying, sir. I don't understand why—"

"Was it a living voice, as far as you could tell?"

"Given the inflections and order of sentiments, I believe it was a recorded message, sir. Or it's being read to us."

"I thought so too."

He moved away from her, back to where McCoy was staring at the screen, eyes wide.

"That's a mighty poetic mouthful," the doctor uttered. "Any idea what it meant?"

"I'd say they're inviting us to get out of their way."

"I told you." Kellen stepped forward, but made no advances toward the helm this time, especially since the guards flanked him snugly now. "Attack them, Kirk. Your chance will slide away under you. Do you see it sliding? I see it."

"Something tells me I'll get another chance, General. Mister Spock, are you reading any shielding on that ship?"

"No, sir," the upper monitor said. "No energy

shields at all, except for the way cloverleaved hull plates fold down."

"Not battle attitude, then," Sulu offered.

"Not ours," Kirk said, stepping down to his command center and slid into his chair. "But we don't know theirs yet, other than the defensive posture we've just seen. Maintain status."

"Aye, sir," said Sulu and Donnier at the same time, and tensed as if they'd realized they were relaxing too much.

Kirk moved back to the rail, where McCoy stood over him. "Opinion?"

"Pretty lofty talk," the doctor said. "But there's a ring to it. I can't put my finger on it."

"Mister Spock?"

By not looking at the monitor, he could imagine that Spock stood up there, next to McCoy, bent over his sensors, adding his deductions to the information being drawn in by the ship's eyes and ears. Spock wouldn't have admitted it, or wanted it said aloud, but there was a lot of intuition in that man.

"There is a common tone in the phrases," Spock said, his voice rough, underscored with physical effort. " 'Witness you conquerors,' for instance. 'Eternal transience,' 'destiny,' 'deathless quest,' and the suggestion that we have been expecting them, that they have been wronged, and that they believe they are returning from somewhere."

"Conclusion?"

"We may have a case of mistaken identity."

"That may not make a difference," McCoy warned. "They're inviting us to leave, remember? They might not take our word for our intentions."

"They can't take anything for anything until we've identified ourselves."

"Captain," Spock's rough voice said from the monitor, "I suggest you answer their immediate request first."

"Set the parameters? Yes . . . I agree."

There it was. The reason he needed Spock here. He hadn't thought of that. Just answer them. The simplest answer had almost slipped by. Set the line of scrimmage before he offered anything else.

"Challenge them!" Kellen insisted. "Demand they stand down and allow us to board and inspect! Then we'll be inside!"

Kirk rubbed his hands and, gazing at the screen, shook his head.

"I think Mister Spock and I have something else in mind. Lieutenant Uhura," he said slowly, "tell them . . . 'no.'"

The
Invasion
Continues
In

STAR TREK
THE NEXT GENERATION®
Invasion!

BOOK TWO

The Solidiers of Fear

by

Dean Wesley Smith

and

Kristine Kathryn Rusch

The message from Starfleet had been curt. Assemble the senior officers. Prepare for a Security One Message at 0900. Picard hadn't heard a Security One Message since the Borg were headed for Earth. The highest-level code. Extreme emergency. Override all other protocols. Abandon all previous orders.

Something serious had happened.

He leaned over the replicator. He had only a moment until the senior officers arrived.

"Earl Grey, hot," he said. The empty space on the replicator shimmered, then a clear glass mug filled with steaming tea appeared. Slipping his thumb through the handle, he gripped the mug by its warm body and took a sip, allowing the liquid to calm him.

He had no clue what this might be about, and that worried him. He always kept abreast of activity in the quadrant. He knew the subtlest changes in the political breeze. The Romulans had been quiet of late; the Cardassians had been cooperating with Bajor. No new ships had been sighted in any sector, and no small rebel groups were taking their rebellions into space. Maybe it was the Klingons?

He should have had an inkling.

His door hissed open and Beverly Crusher came in. Geordi La Forge was beside her. Data followed. The doctor and Geordi looked worried. Data had his usual look of expectant curiosity.

Data sat and turned his back to Geordi so the chief engineer could finish putting his skull cap back in place while they waited.

The door hadn't even had a chance to close before Deanna Troi came in. She was in uniform, a habit she had started just recently. Worf saw her and left his post on the bridge, following her to his position in the meeting room.

Only Commander Riker was missing, and he was the one most needed. Picard couldn't access the message without him.

It was 0859.

Then the door hissed a final time and Will Riker came in. His workout clothes were sweat-streaked, his hair damp. Draped over his shoulder was a towel, which he instantly took off and wadded in a ball in his hand.

"Sorry, sir," he said, "but from your voice, I figured I wouldn't have time to change."

"You were right, Will," Picard said. "We're about to get a message from Starfleet Command. They requested all senior officers be in attendance—"

His desk monitor snapped on with the Federation's symbol, indicating a scrambled communiqué.

"Message sent to Picard, Captain, *U.S.S. Enterprise,* and the senior members of his staff," said the generic female computer voice. "Please confirm identity and status."

Picard placed a hand on the screen on his desk. "Picard, Jean-Luc, Captain, *U.S.S. Enterprise.* Security Code 1-B58A."

The computer beeped. Picard moved away from the screen as Riker put his hand on it. "Riker, William T., First Officer, *U.S.S. Enterprise.* Security Code . . ."

Picard watched as Riker finished his sequence. Picard's palms were damp. He grabbed his mug, but the tea was growing cold. Still, he drank the rest, barely tasting the tea's bouquet.

When the security protocol ended, the Federation symbol disappeared from the screen, replaced by the battle-scarred face of Admiral Kirschbaum. His features had tightened in that emotionless yet urgent expression the oldest—and best—commanders had in times of emergency.

"Jean-Luc. We have no time for discussion. A sensor array at the Furies Point has been destroyed. Five ships of unknown origin are there now, along with what seems to be a small black hole. Two of the ships attacked the Brundage Station. I'm ordering all available ships to the area at top speed."

The Furies Point. Picard needed no more explanation than that. From the serious expressions all around him, he could tell that his staff understood as well.

Picard's hand tightened on the empty glass mug. He set it down before he shattered it with his grip. "We're on our way, Admiral."

"Good." The admiral's mouth tightened. "I hope I don't have to explain—"

"I understand the urgency, Admiral."

"If those ships are what we believe them to be, we're at war, Jean-Luc."

How quickly it happened. One moment he was on the bridge, preparing for the day's duties. The next, this.

"I will act accordingly, Admiral."

The admiral nodded. "You don't have much time, Jean-Luc. I will contact you in one hour with transmissions from the attack on the Brundage outpost. It will give you and your officers some idea of what you are facing."

"Thank you, Admiral," Picard said.

"Godspeed, Jean-Luc."

"And to you," Picard said, but by the time the words were out, the admiral's image had winked away.

Picard felt as if someone had punched him in the stomach.

The Furies.

The rest of the staff looked as stunned as he felt.

Except for Data. When Picard met his gaze, Data said quietly, "It will take us 2.38 hours at Warp Nine to reach Brundage station."

"Then lay in a course, Mister Data, and engage. We don't have time to waste."

The
Invasion
Continues
In

BOOK THREE

Time's Enemy

by

L. A. Graf

"It looks like they're preparing for an invasion," Jadzia Dax said.

Sisko grunted, gazing out at the expanse of dark-crusted cometary ice that formed the natural hull of Starbase 1. Above the curving ice horizon, the blackness of Earth's Oort cloud should have glittered with bright stars and the barely brighter glow of the distant sun. Instead, what it glittered with were the docking lights of a dozen short-range attack ships—older and more angular versions of the *Defiant*—as well as the looming bulk of two Galaxy-class starships, the *Mukaikubo* and the *Breedlove*. One glance had told Sisko that such a gathering of force couldn't have been the random result of ship refittings and shore leaves. Starfleet was preparing for a major encounter with someone. He just wished he knew who.

"I thought we came here to deal with a *non*military

emergency." In the sweep of transparent aluminum windows, Sisko could see Julian Bashir's dark reflection glance up from the chair he'd sprawled in after an glance at the view. Beyond the doctor, the huge conference room was as empty as it had been ten minutes ago when they'd first been escorted into it. "Otherwise, wouldn't Admiral Hayman have asked us to come in the *Defiant* instead of a high-speed courier?"

Sisko snorted. "Admirals never *ask* anything, Doctor. And they never tell you any more than you need to know to carry out their orders efficiently."

"Especially this admiral," Dax added, an unexpected note of humor creeping into her voice. Sisko raised an eyebrow at her, then heard a gravelly snort and the simultaneous hiss of the conference-room door opening. He swung around to see a rangy, long-boned figure in ordinary Starfleet coveralls crossing the room toward them. Dax surprised him by promptly stepping forward, hands outstretched in welcome.

"How have you been, Judith?"

"Promoted." The silver-haired woman's angular face lit with something approaching a sparkle. "It almost makes up for getting this old." She clasped Dax's hands warmly for a moment, then turned her attention to Sisko. "So this is the Benjamin Sisko Curzon told me so much about. It's a pleasure to finally meet you, Captain."

Sisko slanted a wary glance at his science officer. "Um—likewise, I'm sure. Dax?"

The Trill cleared her throat. "Benjamin, allow me to introduce you to Rear Admiral Judith Hayman. She and I—well, she and Curzon, actually—got to know each other on Vulcan during the Klingon peace negotiations several years ago. Judith, this is Captain Benjamin Sisko of *Deep Space Nine,* and our station's chief medical officer, Dr. Julian Bashir."

"Admiral." Bashir nodded crisply.

"Our orders said this was a priority one emergency," Sisko said. "Forgive my bluntness, Admiral, but I assume that means whatever you brought us here to do is urgent."

Hayman's strong face lost its smile. "Possibly," she said. "Although perhaps not urgent in the way we usually think of it."

Sisko scowled. "I've been dragged from my command station without explanation, ordered not to use my own ship under any circumstances, brought to the oldest and least useful starbase in the Federation"— He made a gesture of reined-in impatience at the bleak cometary landscape outside the windows.— "and you're telling me you're not sure how *urgent* this problem is?"

"No one is sure, Captain. That's part of the reason we brought you here." The admiral's voice chilled into something between grimness and exasperation. "What we *are* sure of is that we could be facing potential disaster." She reached into the front pocket of her coveralls and tossed two ordinary-looking datachips onto the conference table. "The first thing I need you and your medical officer to do is review these data records."

"Data records," Sisko repeated, trying for the noncommittal tone he'd perfected over years of trying to deal with the equally high-handed and inexplicable behavior of Kai Wlnn.

"Admiral, forgive us, but we assumed this actually

was an emergency," Julian Bashir explained, in such polite bafflement that Sisko guessed he must be copying Garak's unctuous demeanor. "If so, we could have reviewed your data records ten hours ago. All you had to do was send them to *Deep Space Nine* through subspace channels."

"Too dangerous, even using our most secure codes." The bleak certainty in Hayman's voice made Sisko blink in surprise. "And if you were listening, young man, you'd have noticed that I said this was the *first* thing I needed you to do. Now, would you please sit down, Captain?"

He took the place she indicated at one of the conference table's inset data stations, then waited while she settled Bashir at the station on the opposite side. He noticed she made no attempt to seat Dax, although there were other empty stations available.

"This review procedure is not a standard one," Hayman said, without further preliminaries. "As a control on the validity of some data we've recently received, we're going to ask you to examine ship's logs and medical records without knowing their origin. We'd like your analysis of them. Computer, start data-review programs Sisko-One and Bashir-One."

Sisko's monitor flashed to life, not with pictures but with a thick ribbon of multilayered symbols and abbreviated words, slowly scrolling from left to right. He stared at it for a long, blank moment before a whisper of memory turned it familiar instead of alien. One of the things Starfleet Academy asked cadets to do was determine the last three days of a starship's voyage when its main computer memory had failed. The solution was to reconstruct computer records from each of the ship's individual system buffers—records that looked exactly like these.

"These are multiple logs of buffer output from individual ship systems, written in standard Starfleet machine code," he said. Dax made an interested noise and came to stand behind him. "It looks like someone downloaded the last commands given to life-support, shields, helm, and phaser-bank control. There's another system here, too, but I can't identify it."

"Photon-torpedo control?" Dax suggested, leaning over his shoulder to scrutinize it.

"I don't think so. It might be a sensor buffer." Sisko scanned the lines of code intently while they scrolled by. He could recognize more of the symbols now, although most of the abbreviations on the fifth line still baffled him. "There's no sign of navigations, either—the command buffers in those systems may have been destroyed by whatever took out the ship's main computer." Sisko grunted as four of the five logs recorded wild fluctuations and then degenerated into solid black lines. "And there goes everything else. Whatever hit this ship crippled it beyond repair."

Dax nodded. "It looks like some kind of EM pulse took out all of the ship's circuits—everything lost power except for life-support, and that had to switch to auxiliary circuits." She glanced up at the admiral. "Is that all the record we have, Admiral? Just those few minutes?"

"It's all the record we *trust*," Hayman said enigmatically. "There are some visual bridge logs that I'll show you in a minute, but those could have been tampered with. We're fairly sure the buffer outputs weren't." She glanced up at Bashir, whose usual restless energy had focused down to a silent intensity of concentration on his own data screen. "The medical logs we found were much more extensive. You have time to review the buffer outputs again, if you'd like."

"Please," Sisko and Dax said in unison.

"Computer, repeat data program Sisko-One."

Machine code crawled across the screen again, and this time Sisko stopped trying to identify the individual symbols in it. He vaguely remembered one of his Academy professors saying that reconstructing a starship's movements from the individual buffer outputs of its systems was a lot like reading a symphony score. The trick was not to analyze each line individually, but to get a sense of how all of them were functioning in tandem.

"This ship was in a battle," he said at last. "But I think it was trying to escape, not fight. The phaser banks all show discharge immediately after power fluctuations are recorded for the shields."

"Defensive action," Dax agreed, and pointed at the screen. "And look at how much power they had to divert from life-support to keep the shields going. Whatever was after them was big."

"They're trying some evasive actions now—" Sisko broke off, seeing something he'd missed the first time in that mysterious fifth line of code. Something that froze his stomach. It was the same Romulan symbol that appeared on his command board every time the cloaking device was engaged on the *Defiant*.

"This was a cloaked Starfleet vessel!" He swung around to fix the admiral with a fierce look. "My understanding was that only the *Defiant* had been sanctioned to carry a Romulan cloaking device!"

Hayman met his stare without a ripple showing in her calm competence. "I can assure you that Starfleet isn't running any unauthorized cloaking devices. Watch the log again, Captain Sisko."

He swung back to his monitor. "Computer, rerun data program Sisko-One at one-quarter speed," he said. The five concurrent logs crawled across the screen in slow motion, and this time Sisko focused on the coordinated interactions between the helm and the phaser banks. If he had any hope of identifying the class and generation of this starship, it would be from the tactical maneuvers it could perform.

"Time the helm changes versus the phaser bursts," Dax suggested from behind him in an unusually quiet voice. Sisko wondered if she was beginning to harbor the same ominous suspicion he was.

"I know." For the past hundred years, the speed of helm shift versus the speed of phaser refocus had been the basic determining factor of battle tactics. Sisko's gaze flickered from top line to third, counting off milliseconds by the ticks along the edge of the data record. The phaser refocus rates he found were startlingly fast, but far more chilling was the almost instantaneous response of this starship's helm in its tactical runs. There was only one ship he knew of that had the kind of overpowered warp engines needed to bring it so dangerously close to the edge of survivable maneuvers. And there was only one commander who had used his spare time to perfect the art of skimming along the edge of that envelope, the way the logs told him this ship's commander had done.

This time when Sisko swung around to confront Judith Hayman, his concern had condensed into cold, sure knowledge. "Where did you find these records, Admiral?"

She shook her head. "Your analysis first, Captain. I need your unbiased opinion before I answer any questions or show you the visual logs. Otherwise, we'll never know for sure if these data can be trusted."

Sisko blew out a breath, trying to find words for conclusions he wasn't even sure he believed. "This ship—it wasn't just cloaked like the *Defiant*. It actually *was* the *Defiant*." He heard Dax's indrawn breath. "And when it was destroyed in battle, the man commanding it was me."

The advantage of having several lifetimes of experience to draw on, Jadzia Dax often thought, was that there wasn't much left in the universe that could surprise you. The disadvantage was that you no longer remembered how to cope with surprise. In particular, she'd forgotten the sensation of facing a reality so improbable that logic insisted it could not exist while all your senses told you it did.

Like finding out that the mechanical death throes you had just seen were those of your very own starship.

"Thank you, Captain Sisko," Admiral Hayman said. "That confirms what we suspected."

"But how can it?" Dax straightened to frown at the older woman. "Admiral, if these records are real and not computer constructs—then they must have somehow come from our future!"

"Or from an alternate reality," Sisko pointed out.

He swung the chair of his data station around with the kind of controlled force he usually reserved for the command chair of the *Defiant*. "Just where in space were these transmissions picked up, Admiral?"

Hayman's mouth quirked, an expression Jadzia found unreadable but which Curzon's memories interpreted as rueful. "They weren't—at least not as transmissions. What you're seeing there, Captain, are—"

"—actual records."

It took Dax a moment to realize that those unexpected words had been spoken by Julian Bashir. The elegant human accent was unmistakably his, but the grim tone was not.

"What are you talking about, Doctor?" Sisko demanded.

"These are actual records, taken directly from the *Defiant*." From here, all Dax could see of him was the intent curve of his head and neck as he leaned over his data station. "Medical logs in my own style, made for my own personal use. There's no reason to transmit medical data in this form."

The unfamiliar numbness of surprise was fading at last, and Dax found it replaced by an equally strong curiosity. She skirted the table to join him. "What kind of medical data are they, Julian?"

He threw her a startled upward glance, almost as if he'd forgotten she was there, then scrambled out of his chair to face her. "Confidential patient records," he said, blocking her view of the screen. "I don't think you should see them."

The Dax symbiont might have accepted that explanation, but Jadzia knew the young human doctor too well. The troubled expression on his face wasn't put there by professional ethics. "Are they my records?" she asked, then patted his arm when he winced. "I expected you to find them, Julian. If this was our *Defiant,* then we were probably all on it when it was— I mean, when it *will be*—destroyed."

"What I don't understand," Sisko said with crisp impatience, "is how we can have actual records preserved from an event that hasn't happened yet."

Admiral Hayman snorted. "No one understands that, Captain Sisko—which is why Starfleet Command thought this might be an elaborate forgery." Her piercing gaze slid to Bashir. "Doctor, are you convinced that the man who wrote those medical logs was a *future* you? They're not pastiches put together from bits and pieces of your old records, in order to fool us?"

Bashir shook his head, vehemently. "What these medical logs say that I did—no past records of mine could have been altered enough to mimic that. They have to have been written by a future me." He gave Dax another distressed look. "Although it's a future that I hope to hell never comes true."

"That's a wish the entire Federation is going to share, now that we know these records are genuine." Hayman thumped herself into the head chair at the conference table, and touched the control panel in front of it. One of the windows on the opposite wall obediently blanked into a viewscreen. "Let me show you why."

The screen flickered blue and then condensed into a familiar wide-screen scan of the *Defiant*'s bridge. It was the viewing angle Dax had gotten used to watching in postmission analyses, the one recorded by the official logging sensor at the back of the deck. In this frozen still picture, she could see the outline of Sisko's shoulders and head above the back of his chair, and the top of her own head beyond him, at the helm. The *Defiant*'s viewscreen showed darkness spattered with distant fires that looked a little too large and bright to be stars. The edges of the picture were frayed and spangled with blank blue patches, obscuring the figures at the weapons and engineering consoles. Dax thought she could just catch the flash of Kira's earring through the static.

"The record's even worse than it looks here," Hayman said bluntly. "What you're seeing is a computer reconstruction of the scattered bytes we managed to download from the sensor's memory buffer. All we've got is the five-minute run it recorded just before the bridge lost power. Any record it dumped to the main computer before that was lost."

Sisko nodded, acknowledging the warning buried in her dry words. "So we're going to see the *Defiant*'s final battle."

"That's right." Hayman tapped at her control panel again, and the conference room filled with the sound of Kira's tense voice.

"Three alien vessels coming up fast on vector oh-nine-seven. We can't outrun them." The fires on the viewscreen blossomed into the unmistakable red-orange explosions of warp cores breaching under attack. Dax tried to count them, but there were too many, scattered over too wide a sector of space to keep track of. Her stomach roiled in fierce and utter disbelief. How could so many starships be destroyed this quickly? Had all of Starfleet rallied to fight this hopeless future battle?

"They're also moving too fast to track with our

quantum torpedoes." The sound of her own voice coming from the image startled her. It sounded impossibly calm to Dax under the circumstances. She saw her future self glance up at the carnage on the viewscreen, but from the back there was no way to tell what she thought of it. "Our course change didn't throw them off. They must be tracking our thermal output."

"Drop cloak." The toneless curtness of Sisko's recorded voice told Dax just how grim the situation must be. "Divert all power to shields and phasers."

The sensor image flickered blue and silent for a moment as a power surge ran through it, then returned to its normal tattered state. Now, however, there were three distinct patches of blue looming closer on the future *Defiant*'s viewscreen.

"What's that?" Bashir asked Hayman, pointing.

The admiral grunted and froze the image while she answered him. "That's the computer's way of saying it couldn't match a known image to the visual bytes it got there."

"The three alien spaceships," Dax guessed. "They're not Klingon or Romulan then."

"Or Cardassian or Jem'Hadar," Bashir added quietly.

"As far as we can tell, they don't match any known spacefaring ship design," Hayman said. "That's what worries us."

Sisko leaned both elbows on the table, frowning at the stilled image intently. "You think we're going be attacked by some unknown force from the Gamma Quadrant?"

"Or worse." The admiral cleared her throat, as if her dramatic words had embarrassed her. "You may have heard rumors about the alien invaders that Captain Picard and the *Enterprise* drove off from Brundage Station. From the spectrum of the energy discharges you're going to see when the alien ships fire their phasers at you, the computer thinks there's more than a slight chance that this could be another invasion force."

Dax repressed a shiver at this casual discussion of their catastrophic future. "You think the *Defiant* is going to be destroyed in a future battle with the Furies?"

"We know they think that this region of space once belonged to them," Hayman said crisply. "We know they want it back. And we know we didn't destroy their entire fleet in our last encounter, just the artificial wormhole they used to transport themselves to Furies Point. Given the *Defiant*'s posting near the Bajoran wormhole—" She broke off, waving a hand irritably at the screen. "I'm getting ahead of myself. Watch the rest of the visual log first, then I'll answer your questions." Her mouth jerked downward at one corner. "If I can."

She touched the control panel again to resume the log playback. Almost immediately, the viewscreen flashed with a blast of unusually intense phaser fire.

"Damage to forward shield generators," reported O'Brien's tense voice. "Diverting power from rear shield generators to compensate."

"Return fire!" Sisko's computer-reconstructed figure blurred as he leapt from his captain's chair and went to join Dax at the helm. "Starting evasive maneuvers, program delta!"

More flashes screamed across the viewscreen, obscuring the random jerks and wiggles that the stars made during warp-speed maneuvers. The phaser fire washed the *Defiant*'s bridge in such fierce white light that the crew turned into darkly burned silhouettes. An uneasy feeling grew in Dax that she was watching ghosts rather than real people, and she began to understand Starfleet's reluctance to trust that this log was real.

"Evasive maneuvers aren't working!" Kira sounded both fierce and frustrated. "They're firing in all directions, not just at us."

"Their present course vector will take them past us in twelve seconds, point-blank range," Dax warned. "Eleven, ten, nine . . ."

"Forward shields failing!" shouted O'Brien. Behind his voice the ship echoed with the thunderous sound of vacuum breach. "We've lost sectors seventeen and twenty-one—"

"Six, five, four . . ."

"Spin the ship to get maximum coverage from rear shields," Sisko ordered curtly. *"Now!"*

"Two, one . . ."

Another hull breach thundered through the ship, this one louder and closer than before. The sensor image washed blue and silent again with another power surge. Dax held her breath, expecting the black fade of ship destruction to follow it. To her amazement, however, the blue rippled and condensed back into the familiar unbreached contours of the bridge. Emergency lights glowed at each station, making the crew look shadowy and even more unreal.

"Damage reports," Sisko ordered.

"Hull breaches in all sectors below fifteen," O'Brien said grimly. "We've lost the port nacelle, too, Captain."

"Alien ships are veering off at vector five-sixteen point nine." Kira sounded suspicious and surprised in equal measures. Her silhouette turned at the weapons console, earring glittering. "Sensors report they're still firing phasers in all directions. And for some reason, their shields appear to be failing." A distant red starburst lit the viewscreen, followed by two more. "Captain, you're not going to believe this, but it looks like they just blew up!"

Dax saw herself turn to look at Kira, and for the first time caught a dim glimpse of her own features. As far as she could tell, they looked identical to the ones she'd seen in the mirror that morning. Whatever this future was, it wasn't far away.

"Maybe our phasers caused as much damage as theirs did," she suggested hopefully. "Or more."

"I don't think so." O'Brien's voice was even grimmer now. "I've been trying to put our rear shields back on-line, but something's not right. Something's draining them from the outside." His voice scaled upward in disbelief. "Our main core power's being sucked out right through the shield generators!"

"A new kind of weapon?" Sisko demanded. "Something we can neutralize with our phasers?"

The chief engineer made a startled noise. "No, it's not an energy beam at all. It looks more like—"

At that point, with a suddenness that made Dax's stomach clench, the entire viewscreen went dead. She felt her shoulder and hand muscles tense in involuntary protest, and heard Bashir stir uncomfortably beside her. Sisko cursed beneath his breath.

"I know," Admiral Hayman said dryly. "The main circuits picked the worst possible time to give out. That's all the information we have."

"No, it's not." Julian Bashir's voice sounded bleak rather than satisfied, and Dax suspected he would rather not have had the additional information to give them. "I haven't had a chance to read the majority of these medical logs, but I have found the ones that deal with the aftermath of the battle."

Hayman's startled look at him contained a great deal more respect than it had a few moments before, Dax noticed. "There were logs that talked about the battle? No one wlse noticed that."

"That's because no one else knows my personal abbreviations for the names of the crew," Bashir said simply. "I scanned the records for the ones I thought might have been aboard on this trip. Of the six regular crew, Odo wasn't mentioned anywhere. I'm guessing he stayed back on *Deep Space Nine*. My records for Kira and O'Brien indicate they were lost in some kind of shipboard battle, trying to ward off an invading force. Sisko seems to have been injured then and to have died afterward, but I'm not sure exactly when. And Dax—" He stopped to clear his throat and then resumed. "According to my records, Jadzia suffered so much radiation exposure in the final struggle that she had only a few hours to live. Rather than stay aboard, she took a lifepod and created a diversion for the aliens who were attacking us. That's how the ship finally got away."

"Got away?" Sisko demanded in disbelief. "You mean some of the crew survived the battle we just saw?"

Bashir grimaced. "How do you think those medical logs got written up? I not only survived the battle, Captain, I appear to have lived for a considerable time afterward. There are several years' worth of logs here, if not more."

"Several *years?*" It was Dax's turn to sound incredulous. "You stayed on board the *Defiant* for several years after this battle, Julian? And no one came to rescue you?"

"No."

"That can't be true!" The *Defiant*'s captain vaulted from his chair, as if his churning restlessness couldn't be contained in one place any longer. "Even a totally disabled starship can emit an automatic distress call," he growled. "If no one from Starfleet was alive to respond to it, some other Federation ship should have. *Was our entire civilization destroyed?*"

"No," Hayman said soberly. "The reason's much simpler than that, and much worse. Come with me, and I'll show you."

Cold mist ghosted out at them when the fusion-bay doors opened, making Dax shiver and stop on the theshold. Beside her, she could see Sisko eye the interior with a mixture of foreboding and awe. This immense dark space held a special place in human history, Dax knew. It was the first place where interstellar fusion engines had been fired, the necessary step that eventually led to this solar system's entry into the federation of spacefaring races. She peered through the interior fog of subliming carbon dioxide and water droplets, but aside from a distant tangle of gantry lights, all she could see was the mist.

"Sorry about the condensate," Admiral Hayman said briskly. "We never bothered to seal off the walls, since we usually keep this bay at zero P and T." She palmed open a locker beside the ring doors and handed them belt jets, then launched herself into the mist-filled bay with the graceful arc of a diver. Sisko rolled into the hold with less grace but equal efficiency, followed by the slender sliver of movement that was Bashir. Dax took a deap breath and vaulted after them, feeling the familiar interior lurch of the symbiont in its pouch as their bodies adjusted to the lack of gravitational acceleration.

"This way." The delayed echo of Hayman's voice told Dax that the old fusion bay was widening as they moved farther into the mist, although she could no longer see its ice-carved sides. She fired her belt jets to follow the sound of the admiral's graveled voice, feeling the exposed freckles on her face and neck prickle with cold in the zero-centigrade air. Three silent shadows loomed in the fog ahead of her, backlit by the approaching gantry lights. She jetted into an athletic arc calculated to bring her up beside them.

"So, Admiral, what have you—"

Her voice broke off abruptly, when she saw what filled the space in front of her. The heat of the work lights had driven back the mist, making a halo of clear space around the dark object that was their focus. At first, all she saw was a huge lump of cometary ice, black-crusted over glacial blue gleaming. Then her eye caught a skeletal feathering of old metal buried in that ice, and followed it around an oddly familiar curve until it met another, more definite sweep of metal. Beyond that lay a stubby wing, gashed through with ice-filled fractures. She took in a deep, icy breath as the realization hit her.

"That's the *Defiant!*"

"Or what's left of her." Sisko's voice rang grim echoes off the distant walls of the hold. Now that she had recognized the ship's odd angle in the ice, Dax could see that he was right. The port nacelle was sheared off entirely, and a huge torpedo-impact crater had exploded into most of the starboard hull and decking. Phaser burns streaked the *Defiant*'s flanks, and odd unfamiliar gashes had sliced her to vacuum in several places.

She glanced across at Hayman. "Where was this found, Admiral?"

"Right here in Earth's Oort cloud," the admiral said, without taking her eyes from the half-buried starship. "A mining expedition from the Pluto LaGrangian colonies, out prospecting for water-cored comets, found it two days ago after a trial phaser blast. They recognized the Starfleet markings and called us, but it was too fragile to free with phasers out there. We had to bring it in and let the cometary matrix melt around it."

"But if it was that fragile—" Dax frowned, her scientist's brain automatically calculating metal fatigue under deep-space conditions, while her emotions kept insisting that what she was seeing was impossible. "It must have been buried inside that comet for thousands of years!"

"Almost five millennia," Hayman agreed. "According to thermal spectroscopy of the ice around it, and radiometric dating of the—er—the organic contents of the ship."

"You mean, the bodies," Bashir said, breaking his stark silence at last.

"Yes." Hayman jetted toward the far side of the ice-sheathed ship, where a brighter arc of lights was trained on the *Defiant*'s main hatch. "There's a slight discrepancy between the individual radiocarbon ages of the two survivors, apparently as a result of—"

"—differential survival times." The doctor finished the sentence so decisively that Dax suspected he'd already known that from his medical logs. She glanced at him as they followed Hayman toward the ship, puzzled by the sudden urgency in his voice. "How much of a discrepancy in ages was there? More than a hundred years?"

"No, about half that." The admiral glanced over her shoulder, the quizzical look back in her eyes. "Humans don't generally live long enough to survive each other by more than a hundred years, Doctor."

Dax heard the quick intake of Bashir's breath that told her he was startled. "Both bodies you found were human?"

"Yes." Hayman paused in front of the open hatch, blocking it with one long arm when Sisko would have jetted past her. "I'd better warn you that, aside from microsampling for radiocarbon dates, we've left the remains just as they were found in the medical bay. One was in stasis, but the other—wasn't."

"Understood." Sisko pushed past her into the dim hatchway, the cold control of his voice telling Dax how much he hated seeing the wreckage of the first ship he'd ever commanded. She let Bashir enter next, sensing the doctor's fierce impatience from the way his fingers had whitened around his tricorder. When she would have jetted after him, Hayman touched her shoulder and made her pause.

"I know your new host is a scientist, Dax. Does that mean you've already guessed what happened here?"

Dax gave the older woman a curious look. "It seems fairly self-evident, Admiral. In some future timeline, the *Defiant* is going to be destroyed in a battle so enormous that it will get thrown back in time and halfway across the galaxy. That's why no one could come to rescue Julian."

Hayman nodded, her voice deepening a little. "I just want you to know before you go in—right now, Starfleet's highest priority is to avoid entering that timeline. At all costs." She gave Dax's shoulder a final squeeze, then released her. "Remember that."

"I will." Although she managed to keep her tone as level as always, somewhere inside Dax a tendril of doubt curled from symbiont to host. Curzon's stored memories told Jadzia that when he knew her, this silver-haired admiral had been one of Starfleet's most pragmatic and imperturbable starship captains. Any future that could put that kind of intensity into Hayman's voice wasn't one Dax wanted to think about.

Now she was going to see it.

Inside the *Defiant,* stasis generators made a trail of red lights up the main turbolift shaft, and Dax suspected the half-visible glimmer of their fields was all that kept its crumbling metal walls intact. It looked as though this part of the ship had suffered one of the hull breaches O'Brien had reported, or some even bigger explosion. The turbolift car was a collapsed cage of oxidized steel resin and ceramic planks. Dax eased herself into the open shaft above it, careful not to touch anything as she jetted upward.

"Captain?" she called up into the echoing darkness.

"On the bridge." Sisko's voice echoed oddly off the muffling silence of the stasis fields. Dax boosted herself to the top of the turbolift shaft and then angled her jets to push through the shattered lift doors. Heat lamps had been set up here to melt away the ice still engulfing the *Defiant*'s navigations and science stations. The powerful buzz of their filaments and the constant drip and sizzle of melting water filled the bridge with noise. Sisko stood alone in the midst of it, his face set in stony lines. She guessed that Bashir had headed immediately for the starship's tiny medical bay.

"It's hard to believe it's really five thousand years old," Dax said, hearing the catch in her own voice. The familiar black panels and data stations of the bridge had suffered less damage than the rest of the ship. Except for the sparkle of condensation off their dead screens, they looked as if all they needed was an influx of power to take up their jobs again. She glanced toward the ice-sheathed science station and shivered. Only two days ago, she'd helped O'Brien install a new sensor array in that console. She could still see the red gleam of its readouts beneath the ice—brand-new sensors that were now far older than her own internal symbiont.

Dax shook off the unreality of it and went to join Sisko at the command chair. Seeing the new sensor array had given her an idea. "Can you tell if there are any unfamiliar modifications on the bridge?" she asked the captain, knowing he had probably memorized the contours of his ship in a way she hadn't. "If so, they may indicate how far in our future this *Defiant* was when it got thrown back in time."

Sisko swung in a slow arc, his jets hissing. "I don't see anything unfamiliar. This could be the exact ship we left back at *Deep Space Nine.* If the Furies are going to invade, I'd guess it's going to be soon."

Hayman grunted from the doorway. "That's exactly the kind of information we needed you to give us, Captain. Now all we need to know is where and when they'll come, so we can be prepared to meet them."

"And this—this ghost from the future." Sisko reached out a hand as if to touch the *Defiant*'s dead helm, then dropped it again when it only stirred up the warning luminescence of a stasis field. "You think this can somehow help us find out—"

The chirp of his commbadge interrupted him. "Bashir to Sisko."

The captain frowned and palmed his badge. "Sisko here. Have you identified the bodies, Doctor?"

"Yes, sir." There was a decidedly odd note in Bashir's voice, Dax thought. Of course, it couldn't be easy examining your own corpse, or those of your closest friends. "The one in the ship's morgue sustained severe trauma before it hit stasis, but it's still recognizable as yours. There wasn't much left of the other, but based on preliminary genetic analysis of some bone fragments, I'll hazard a guess that it used to be me." Dax heard the sound of a slightly unsteady breath. "There's something else down here, Captain. Something I think you and—and Jadzia ought to see."

She exchanged speculative looks with Sisko. For all his youth, there wasn't much that could shatter Julian Bashir's composure when it came to medical matters. "We're on our way," the captain told him. "Sisko out."

Diving back into the shattered darkness of the main

turbolift, with the strong lights of the bridge now behind her, Dax could see what she'd missed on the way up—the pale, distant quiver of emergency lights from the *Defiant*'s tiny sickbay on the next deck down. She frowned and followed Sisko down the clammy service corridor toward it. "Is the ship's original power still on down here?" she demanded incredulously.

From the darkness behind her, she could hear Hayman snort. "Thanks to the size of the warp core on this overpowered attack ship of yours, yes. With all the other systems shut down except for life-support, the power drain was reduced to a trickle. Our engineers think the lights and equipment in here could have run for another thousand years." She drifted to a gentle stop beside Dax and Sisko in the doorway of the tiny medical bay. "A tribute to Starfleet engineering. And to you too, apparently, Doctor Bashir."

The young physician looked up with a start from where he leaned over one of his two sickbay stasis units, as if he'd already forgotten that he'd summoned them here. The glow of thin green emergency lighting showed Dax the unaccustomed mixture of helplessness and self-reproach on his face.

"Right now, I'm not sure that's anything to be proud of," he said, sounding almost angry. His gesture indicated the stasis unit below him, which Dax now saw had been remodeled into an odd mass of pumps and power generators topped with a glass box. A fierce shiver of apprehension climbed up the freckles on her spine and made her head ache. "Why haven't you people done anything about this?"

Admiral Hayman's steady glance traveled from him

to Dax, and then back again. "Because we were waiting for you."

That was all the confirmation Dax needed. She pushed past Sisko, and was startled to find herself dropped abruptly to the floor when the sickbay's artificial gravity caught her. Just a little under one Earth standard, she guessed from the feel of it—she felt oddly light and off-balance as she joined Bashir on the other side of that carefully remodeled medical station.

"Julian, is it . . . ?"

His clear brown eyes met hers across the misted top of the box. "I'm afraid so," he said softly, and moved his hand. Below where the warmth of his skin had penetrated the stasis-fogged glass, the mist had cleared a little. It was enough to show Dax what Bashir had already seen—the unmistakable gray-white mass of a naked Trill symbiont, immersed in brine that held a frozen glitter of bioelectric activity.

She had to take a deep breath before she located her voice, but this time her symbiont's long years of experience stood her in good stead. "Well," she said slowly, gazing down at the part of herself that was now immeasurably older. "Now I know why I'm here."

YR1,DY6,2340

Patient immobile + unresponsive. Limited contact + manipulation of subject due to fragile physical state and possible radiation damage, no invasive px/tx until vitals, Tokal-Benar's stabilize. Fluid isoboramine values <47%, biospectral scan-

cortical activity < prev. observed norm, ion con-
centration still unstable. (see lab/chem results,
atta) No waste products yet; adjusted nutrient mix
+10% in hopes of improving uptake. Am begin-
ning to fear I can't really keep it alive after all.

Staring down into the milky shadows of the suspen-
sion tank, Julian Bashir blinked away the image of
those old medical records and trailed a hand across
the invisible barrier separating the two realities. The
stasis field pricked at his palm like a swarm of sleepy
bees. "I guess I was wrong."

"Does that mean you don't think it's still alive?"

Bashir jerked his head up, embarrassment at being
overheard smothering under a flush of guilt as soon as
the meaning of Hayman's words sank in. He pulled
his hand away from the forcefield, then ended up
clenching it at his side when he could find nothing else
to do with it. "No, I'm fairly certain it's still living."
At least, that's what the readouts frozen beneath the
stasis field's glow seemed to indicate. "It was alive
when the field was activated five thousand years ago,
at any rate. I can't tell anything else about its condition without examining it in real time." Although the
thought of holding the orphaned symbiont in his
hands made his throat hurt.

Across the table from him, Hayman folded her
arms and frowned down at the shimmering box. The
watery green of the emergency lights turned her eyes
an emotionless bronze, and painted her hair with
neon streaks where there should have been silver.

"Assuming it's in fairly stable condition, what equipment would you need to transfer this symbiont into a Trill host?"

The question struck him like a blow to the stomach. "You can't be serious!" But he knew she was, knew it the very moment she asked. "Admiral, you can't just change Trill symbionts the way you would a pair of socks! There are enormous risks unless very specific compatibility requirements are met—"

"What rejection?" Hayman freed one hand to wave at Dax, standing silently beside her. "It's the same symbiont she has inside her right now!"

It occurred to Bashir, not for the first time, that he didn't like this woman very much. He couldn't imagine what Curzon Dax had ever seen in her. "It's a genetically identical symbiont that is *five thousand years* out of balance with Jadzia! For all we know, the physiological similarities between the two Daxes could make it even harder for Jadzia to adjust to the psychological differences." Dax herself had withdrawn from the discussion almost from the beginning. She'd turned her attention instead toward the naked symbiont in its stasis-blurred coffin, and Bashir wondered which of her many personalities was responsible for the eerie blend of affection and grief he could read in her expression. He wished he could make Hayman understand the implications of toying with a creature that was truly legion. "These are *lives* we're talking about, Admiral, not inconveniences. Any one of the three could die if we attempt what you're suggesting."

Hayman glared at him with that chill superiority Bashir had learned to recognize as a line officer's way of saying that doctors only earned their MDs because they hadn't the stomach for regular Starfleet. "If we don't find out who carved up the *Defiant* and pitched her back into prehistory," she told him coldly, "millions of people could die."

He clenched his jaw, but said nothing. *That's the difference between us,* he thought with sudden clarity. As regular military, Hayman had the luxury of viewing sentient lives in terms of numbers and abstractions—saving one million mattered more than saving one, and whoever ended the war with the most survivors won. As a doctor, he had only the patient, and even a million patients came down to a single patient, handled over and over again. No amount of arithmetic comparison could make him disregard that duty. And thank God for that.

Hayman made a little noise of annoyance at his silence, and shifted her weight to a more threatening stance. "Do I have to make this an order, Dr. Bashir?"

He lifted his chin defiantly. "As the senior medical officer present, sir, Starfleet regulations allow me to countermand any order you give that I feel is not in the best interests of my patient." He flicked a stiff nod at the stasis chamber. "This is one of those orders."

Surprise and anger flashed scarlet across her cheeks. For one certain, anguished moment, Bashir saw himself slammed into a Starfleet brig for insubordination while Hayman did whatever she damn well pleased with the symbiont. It wasn't how he wanted things to go, but it also wasn't the first time that a clear vision of the consequences came several seconds behind his words. He opened his mouth to recant them—at least in part—just as the admiral turned to scowl at Sisko. "Captain, would you like to speak with your doctor?"

The captain lifted his eyebrows in deceptively mild inquiry. "Why?" He moved a few steps away from the second examining bed, the one that held the delicate tumble of bones that Bashir had scrupulously not dealt with after identifying whose they were. "He seems to be doing just fine to me."

Hayman blew an exasperated breath, and her frustration froze into a cloud of vapor on the air. Like dragon's breath. "Do I have to remind you people that you were brought here so Starfleet could help you avert your own deaths?"

"Not if it means treating Jadzia or either of the Daxes as a sacrifice," Bashir insisted.

Dax stirred at the foot of the examining table. "May I say something?"

Bashir kept his eyes locked on Hayman's, refusing the admiral even that small retreat. "Please do."

"Julian, I appreciate your concern for my welfare, and for everything you must have gone through to keep the symbiont alive all this time . . ." Dax reached out to spread her cool hand over his, and Bashir realized with a start that he'd slipped his hand onto the stasis field again. "But I don't think this is really your decision to make."

He felt his heart seize into a fist. "Jadzia—"

"Dax." She joggled his wrist gently as though trying

to gain his attention. "I'm *Dax,* Julian. *This*—" She patted his hand on the top of the tank, and he looked where she wanted despite himself. *"This* is Dax, too." The pale gray blur was nestled in its bed of liquid like a just-formed infant in its mother's womb. "I trust you enough to be certain you didn't do this as some sort of academic exercise. Preserving the symbiont must have been something you knew for a fact that I wanted—that *Dax* wanted. And the only reason I can think of that I'd be willing to live in a tank like this for so many hundreds of years is the chance to warn us about what happened—to prevent it in any way I can."

Sisko came across the room, stopping behind Dax as though wanting to take her by the shoulders even though he didn't reach out. "We don't know that for certain, old man. And if we lose both you *and* the symbionts testing out a theory . . ." His voice trailed off, and Bashir found he wasn't reassured to know that Sisko was just as afraid of failure as he was.

"We're only talking about a temporary exchange," Dax persisted. "Julian has obviously managed to re-create a symbiont breeding pool well enough to sustain my current symbiont for the hour or two we'll need."

But being correct about the timeframe didn't mean she was correct about the procedure. "There's still the psychological aspect," he said softly. "We don't know what the isolation has done to the symbiont's mental stability." His hand stiffened unwillingly on the top of the tank. "Or what that might do to yours."

Dax caught up his gaze with hers, the barest hint of a shared secret coloring her smile as she took his arms to hold him square in front of her, like a mother reassuring her child. "I know for a fact that even six months of exposure to mental instability can't destroy a Trill with seven lifetimes of good foundation. Six hours with some other aspect of myself isn't going to unhinge me." She let her smile widen, and it did nothing to calm the churning in his stomach. "You'll see."

"If you're not willing to perform the procedure, Doctor, I'm sure there are other physicians aboard this starbase who will."

Anger flared in him as though Hayman had thrown gasoline across a spark. Dax's hands tightened on his elbows, startling him into silence as she whirled to snap, "Judith, don't! I won't have him blackmailed into doing this."

The admiral's eyes widened, more surprised than irritated by the outburst, but she crossed her arms without commenting. A more insecure gesture than before, Bashir noticed. He was secretly glad. He didn't like being the only one unsure of himself at a time like this.

"What if there were some other way?" he asked Dax. She opened her mouth to answer, and he pushed on quickly, "Symbionts can communicate with one another without sharing a host, can't they? When they're in the breeding pools back on Trill—when you're in the breeding pools with them?"

The thought had apparently never occurred to her.

One elegant eyebrow lifted, and Dax's focus shifted to somewhere invisible while she considered. "It doesn't transfer all the symbiont's knowledge the way a joining does," she acknowledged after a moment. "But, yes, direct communication is possible."

A little pulse of hope pushed at his heart. "And in a true joining, Jadzia wouldn't retain any of the symbiont's memories, anyway, once the symbiont was removed."

Dax nodded thoughtfully. "That's true."

"So what harm is there in trying this first?"

"Trying what first?" Hayman's confidence must not have been too badly damaged, because the impatient edge to her voice returned easily enough. "What are you two talking about?"

Bashir looked over Dax's shoulder at the admiral, schooling the dislike from his voice in an effort to sound more professional. "When they aren't inside a host, Trill symbionts use electrochemical signals to communicate with one another through the liquid they live in. Even a hosted symbiont can make contact with the others, if its host is first submerged in the fluid pool." He glanced aside at the tank while his thoughts raced a dozen steps ahead. "If we can replicate the nutrient mixture that's been supporting the symbiont, and fill a large enough receptacle, I think the Daxes should be able to . . ." He hesitated slightly, then fell back on the easiest word. ". . . talk to each other without having to remove Jadzia's current symbiont."

Hayman chewed the inside of her lip. "We could question this unhosted symbiont that way? It could talk to us through Dax?"

"Through Jadzia," Bashir corrected automatically, then felt heat flash into his cheeks at Hayman's reproving scowl. "Yes, we could."

"Julian's right." Dax saved him from the rest of the admiral's disapproval. "I think this will work."

"And if it doesn't work?" Hayman fixed Bashir with a suspicious glare, as if expecting him to lie to her. "What are our chances of losing the symbiont?"

"I don't know," he admitted. He wished the truth weren't so unhelpful. "I don't know how fragile it is, how much radiation damage it may have sustained back then. It may not live beyond removal of the stasis field, and I don't know what effect physically moving it from one tank to another might have." He looked into Dax's eyes so that she could see he was being absolutely honest, as a doctor and as her friend. "I do know it will be less traumatic than trying to accomplish a joining under these conditions."

Dax nodded her understanding with a little smile, then squeezed his arms once before releasing him to fold her own hands behind her back. "I think this will be our best option."

"All right, then." Hayman flashed Bashir an appreciative grin, all his sins just that quickly forgiven now that she had what she wanted. Bashir wondered if that was supposed to make him feel as guilty as it did. "Let's give this a try. Lieutenant"—She gathered both Dax and Sisko to her side with a wave of one hand.—"you and the captain can tell me how much fluid and what size tank we'll need, then help me get it all down here. Doctor, wake up the symbiont." She leaned across the tank to clap him manfully on the shoulder, and Bashir found he didn't like the contact. "Looks like it's time to finish what you started."

The
Invasion
Continues
In

BOOK FOUR

The Final Fury

by

Dafydd Ab Hugh

There is no fear. There is no pain. There is no emotion . . . let it fade and disappear. Pure logic: logic fills your brain. Thought is symbol, and logic gives you complete power over all symbols.

The meditation helped, but Lieutenant Tuvok still found himself caught in the grip of illogical emotion, the DNA memory of a hundred thousand years ago perturbing his endocrine system, triggering the release of Vulcan vidrenalase, which affects Vulcans as adrenaline affects humans. Tuvok trembled; he could not control the fine motor skills. It was the best he could do to maintain a veneer of logic and rationality across a sea of barbaric feelings and impulses.

He stumbled along behind the Fury, behind the captain and Neelix, through the warm, moist tunnel. Even in his nightmare state, he could not help but notice that it was like a return up the birth canal; but rather than fascinate him, as it should have, the image filled Tuvok with the unaccustomed *emotions* of loathing and disgust.

Like the impulse to kill the interlocutor, Navdaq, and every other demon on the planet, all twenty-seven billion of them. It was worse than the *pon farr*—at least the mating madness was carefully channeled by ritual. Tuvok had no ritual to deal with the primitive emotions that these creatures stirred in him. Only his meditation.

Tuvok was not bothered by the darkness of the corridor, nor by what the captain considered to be disturbing architecture: angles that did not quite meet at ninety degrees but looked as though they ought to, tricks of perspective that made walls or ceilings seem closer or farther than they were, or strange tilts that threw off a human's sense of balance, which was tied so completely into visual cuing.

But he was disturbed by the sudden intrusion of a long-forgotten cavern in the Vulcan mind, the genetic memory of defeat and slavery so complete and remote it left no trace in the historical record, which was thought to have stretched back farther in time than the conquest.

Evidently not, thought Tuvok, clutching at the logical train of thought; *apparently, there are significant gaps in the historical record. I must write a report for the* Vulcan Journal of Archeology and Prehistory. Then he shuddered.

In our innermost beings, we are not very different from Romulans after all, he thought. With bitterness—another emotion; they came thick and fast now.

In fact, Tuvok realized they would never stop . . .

not until he forced himself to confront the Fury. Gritting his teeth against the terrors, Tuvok increased his stride until he stood but an arm's length behind Navdaq; then with a quick move, before he could disgrace his race further by losing his nerve, Tuvok reached out and caught Navdaq by the shoulder, spinning the creature around to face him.

Tuvok looked directly into Navdaq's face—and felt an abyss open inside him to swallow his heart.

I know you! he thought, unable to keep excitement and emotion even out of his thoughts. *You are Ok'San, the Overlord!*

Ok'San was the most despised of all Vulcan demons, for she was the mother of all the rest. The mythology was so ancient that it was consciously known only to a few scholars; even Tuvok knew only dimly of the stories, and only because of his interest in Vulcan history.

But all Vulcans knew Ok'San but refused to think of her, for she represented *loss of control* and *loss of reason:* there was little else that a sane Vulcan feared apart from the loss of everything it meant to be a Vulcan: logic, control, order, and reason.

In demonic mythology, Ok'San crept through the windows at night, the hot, dry Vulcan night, and crouched on the chests of her "chosen" dreamers: poets, composers, authors, philosophers, scientists, political analysts . . . the very people whose creativity was slowly knitting together the barbaric strands of early Vulcan society into a vision of a logical tomorrow, who groped for shreds of civilization in the horror of Vulcan's yesterday.

She crouched on a dreamer's chest, leaned over his writhing body, and pressed her lips against his. She spat into his mouth, and the spittle rolled down his throat and filled his heart with the *Fury of Vulcan.*

The Fury of Vulcan manifested as a berserker rage that flooded the victim and drove him to paroxysms of horrific violence that defied the descriptive power of logic.

Tuvok had tried to contemplate what must pass through a Vulcan's mind to drive him to kill his own family with a blunt stick, striking their heads hard enough to crush bone and muscle and still have force enough to destroy the brain. In one of the few instances of the Fury of Vulcan to be well recorded by the testimony of many witnesses, a Vulcan hunter-warrior named Torkas of the Vehm, perhaps eighty thousand years ago, grabbed up a leaf-bladed Vulcan Toth spear and set out after the entire population of his village. He managed to kill ninety-seven and wound an additional fourteen, six critically, before he was killed.

Tuvok had always believed Ok'San was the personification of the violent, nearly sadistic rage that filled the hearts of Vulcans before Surak. The Fury of Vulcan always seemed like a disease of the nervous system; yet it was curious that there were no recorded instances of the Fury within historical times . . . not a one.

Diseases do not die out; and it was unlikely in the extreme that primitive Vulcans who had neither logic nor medical science could have destroyed the virus that caused the Fury.

It was an enigma, until now.